*For
Dot Ridolphi*

MW01234648

*Blessings,
Ruric E Wheeler*

All Because of
POLLY

Ruric E. Wheeler

SPG
SELAH PUBLISHING GROUP

Printed in the United States of America

Publishing services by Selah Publishing Group, LLC, Arizona. The views expressed or implied in this work do not necessarily reflect those of Selah Publishing Group.

ISBN 1-58930-064-5
Library of Congress Control Number: 2002109116

Prologue

God is so good! In fact, He has been so good to me that I just have to tell you about it. Also, God loves you. How do I know? If God could love me, a stubborn, cantankerous, self-centered, selfish bumpkin from the hills of Kentucky, then God could love anyone.

God works in mysterious ways. He knew my tendency for getting into trouble, so He caused me to fall in love with a cute freckle-faced twelve-year-old girl, who was a dedicated Christian. In my heart I kept her on a pedestal. I attended Sunday school, church, and a youth program on Sunday night just to be near Polly. I wonder what I would have become in life if there had been no Polly.

God had difficulty getting me to cooperate. He wanted me to be in His will so He could provide for me a wonderful life, but I was stubborn. So He had to temper my life for service in His kingdom. How? Have you ever been madly in love with your next-door neighbor, who has a steady boy friend? I tell you, it is terrible.

Polly always encouraged me to make a greater effort to be in God's will. However, I continued to follow my own selfish desires. One day I did turn my problems and my life over to the Lord. No longer was my love for Polly a burden. Being in God's will is the greatest thing that can happen to anyone. Only then can one have true happiness and satisfaction.

I invite you to travel with me back to the 1930's and let me introduce this cute freckle-faced girl. Maybe she will affect your life the same way she affected mine.

Buddy Baskins

Two Boxes In a Trunk

Time changes everything. It moves like a storm in the middle of the night, wiping away whatever is in its path. Things dear to our hearts such as the old home place, where we enjoyed Mom's cooking and Dad's big hugs, are a part of the past. My name is Buddy Baskins, and my job now is to get everything ready for the big auction; first the furniture and then the house will be sold to the highest bidder. Prior to the auction I must sort everything into items to be sold, things to take to Mother, and an abundance of junk to be thrown away. The U-haul trailer is full of items Mother will treasure as she lives her last years with my sister.

My last and most difficult task is to sort through the old trunk in Mom and Dad's bedroom. Mother said, "You can have what you want from the trunk; throw the rest away." Through the years it has been my impression that this old trunk must contain a collection of very special things.

As I open the trunk I see three big ledgers, records of charge accounts at Dad's old general merchandise store, accounts unpaid through all these many years, along with other business records. My first reaction is, "This is a lot of junk." Reaching deep into the trunk I find my old school records wrapped in brown paper. An old suit box contains my army jacket, cap and other reminders of my military service. There is an old Bible from teenage years. Something else remains in the bottom of the trunk. "Oh no!" I moan. I can't believe my eyes. "Surely not!" Finally I push things aside and look again. Two large identical cigar boxes are stuffed with papers and mementos and tightly tied with cotton fishing line.

I realize then that Mom and Dad saved this old trunk just for me. In it are items to remind me of their teachings about life. The material in this trunk would mean little to an outsider, but I knew the thinking of Mom and Dad about each item in the trunk.

I glance again at the two cigar boxes, and my eyes fill with tears. Can I be sure I recognize these boxes? Can I trust my eyes? It has been a long, long time. Can this really be the boxes that disappeared many years ago?

I begin talking to myself, looking around sheepishly to be sure that I am alone. Then I start talking to Mom and Dad even though they are both gone.

Yes Mom, yes Dad, I remember the lessons you taught me during the Great Depression such as "Never buy anything until you have the money to pay for it."

I know now that we were very poor during that time, but because of your love my sister and I did not realize we were poor. Dad, we thought it was great when you were a share-cropper; we enjoyed riding on the drag as the mule pulled it over the dusty field. Mom did not enjoy getting the dust off our faces. One year you had a great crop of tobacco. You had enough money to accomplish your dream. You wanted to become a merchant following in the footsteps of your grandfather. He had returned home from the Civil War with several months of back pay, which he prudently used to establish a store and mill. Old Hiram had been a success. You felt you could do the same, so you purchased a store at Defries, Kentucky.

It was difficult financially getting started in the merchandising business, but you were very frugal. By flattening pasteboard boxes, you covered the walls and ceiling of the side room of the store (actually designed for storing fence and cow feed) to make living quarters. We lived in three rooms separated by cloth curtains, with the walls and ceiling papered with newspapers. I longed for the time when I would go to school so I could read the walls and ceiling of my room.

One night, I heard Mom crying and Dad, saying, "Don't worry, honey, we will make it." It had something to do with the closing of all the banks in the United States. This, I learned later, was the beginning of the Great Depression. Many people felt they would lose all the money they had in their local banks. For the store, there were bills due on goods purchased, but there was no way to get money from the bank to pay the bills. When I went to sleep that night, you were trying to determine how you would keep the store open. When I got up in the morning, there were smiles on your faces. You had a plan. You would announce to your customers and to the wholesale companies that you were going on a "cash basis." As soon as you sold enough in the store to have cash available, you would place an order for more merchandise, paying cash for it when it arrived. The wholesale companies would just have to trust you for what you owed for past orders. Someday, you would pay all of your debts even if the banks did not open. The main thing now was keeping the store open so you could serve the good people in the community and at the same time feed the family.

Later you had to change your plans. Many families in rural areas faced starvation. With food in the store you could not let people starve, so you made exceptions to your all-cash policy. Families were allowed to buy food and put the cost on a charge account (a promise to pay later). You knew you would never collect most of these debts. However, the Lord blessed your concern for people, and your business increased enough to take care of the bad debts, still recorded in the ledgers.

I remember the greatest disadvantage of living in the country during this period was the lack of adequate medical care. We had been fortunate and had not had serious need for a doctor, but one day you, Mom, were very ill: measles followed by a miscarriage. I did not know what a miscarriage was, but it had to be something bad because you were really sick.

I was playing with my make-believe car beneath the store building when I heard two women talking. One said, "She is going to die." The other replied, "Yes, I don't believe she will last through the day." I suddenly realized they were talking about my mom. What would Sis and I do if you died? Would we get another mother? I was completely confused.

Dad drove to the nearest city, Glasgow, and arranged for a doctor to come to examine you. You seemed to be in a coma. Your heart was barely beating. The doctor tried to stimulate your heartbeat, but the medicine he had with him would not work. Then, the doctor went into the store and asked, "Does anyone know where I can find some whiskey? That woman is going to die if we do not find a stimulant for her heart."

No one said anything. However, in less than five minutes a hand reached around the back door and left a bottle of whiskey. The doctor tasted the whiskey and proclaimed, "This is the strongest bootleg whiskey I have ever tasted."

No one knew where the whiskey came from or who left it, but I had a good idea. Alto and Otis, who lived with their parents as close neighbors, were rumored to have a moonshine still way back in the woods near Green River. I had heard this in the store. Most people thought they made their living by hunting, trapping, and fishing. They were experts at this trade. However, some guessed that they had a much more profitable sideline. I was certain it was Otis who had helped you, because Otis was my friend. He was always making whistles and slingshots and bringing me chestnuts and hickory nuts. My thoughts were, "Even if he is a bootlegger, he likes little boys. I'm glad Otis is my friend."

The prescription – one-fourth cup of whiskey, three tablespoons of honey, and one- half cup of water, every hour – worked miracles. In less than twenty-four hours you were feeling better. It took you another twenty-four hours to realize the medicine you were taking was whiskey, which you hated with a passion. You declared, "I will not take that stuff. I will get well without it." And you did.

Many have commented that the Great Depression built strong individuals, characterized by hard work, integrity, and a concern for others. Undoubtedly the Great Depression affected my life, but that which is found in the two cigar boxes better describes that which molded my life into the person I am today.

Yes Mom, yes Dad, you did a good job teaching me that education was important. Remember when I was always asking the question, "When will I be old enough to go to school?" Finally that day arrived. You dressed me in a freshly ironed, handmade playsuit. It consisted of a top with two buttons at the front and two buttons at the rear. The short pants were buttoned to the two buttons in the front for front-end emergencies and to the two buttons in the back for back-end emergencies.

The first half-day at the little one room school went well, but after eating my lunch, I needed to unbutton the front two buttons of my suit. I headed toward the two-holer about which my sister had repeated at least thirty times, "That one is for boys."

When I finally re-buttoned my two front buttons and stepped out of the privy, there was Leroy Scoggins, a big eighth grader, in the middle of my path.

"Fancy Pants," said Leroy as he grabbed my arm. "The boys are having a meeting over behind that clump of bushes."

He was right. Just about all of the boys in the school were there waiting for me, and it was not even my birthday.

"Fancy Pants," said Leroy. "Can you fight?" Now I'd had a few skirmishes with my sister before running away from her wrath, but I decided I had never really had a fight so I said, "No."

"Well, we are going to teach you to fight. Who wants to fight Fancy Pants?" yelled Leroy.

Immediately each of the other four beginning students raised his hand. They knew they were going to have to fight someone, and they recognized a pushover.

"Okay, Fats, give Fancy Pants a good whipping," ordered Leroy.

Before a fight the older boys would bet their marbles on their selected winner. However, no one wanted to wager a marble on Fancy Pants. Thank goodness, Fats was a bit slow. He was big for his age, but he had also eaten too much hog meat and was truly fat. If Fats had hit me with one of his wild swings, I would surely have been a goner. However, I had developed a quickness from practice dodging my sister. So Fats could not catch me. Finally, he got hold of my arm, threw me to the ground, and sat on me. Leroy declared Fats to be the winner. My only suffering was due to a few short jabs to the ribs as Fats sat on me.

"Fancy Pants, look at George Kersley," ordered Leroy.

I looked at George. He was the meanest looking fifth grader I had ever seen.

"Fancy Pants, if you tell the teacher about this fight, or if you tell your sister about this fight, or if you tell your mom and dad about this fight, tomorrow you will have to fight George."

"I won't, I won't," I cried as I rushed toward the schoolhouse after they had brushed some of the dirt from my freshly starched playsuit.

My second day at school was as bad as the first. I was dressed in another clean four-buttoned playsuit. I knew well what was going to happen down behind the outhouse. Somehow, I thought that things would be easier if I were not so clean. There was a big mud hole on the way to school, and I decided to wade in it, much to the unhappiness of my sis. In trying to get me out of the mud, she got a bit of mud on one of her legs. She was really angry, and left with the promise that she was going to tell you when she got home. All of a sudden, I realized I was too dirty to go to school, and all I knew to do was cry. There I was, crying in a mud hole. When

I arrived at school, the teacher was unhappy with my appearance and sent me home.

Dad, you had already heard the report that your son was standing in a mud hole, crying. I expected a good whipping. However, after I explained that the boys laughed at my clothes, you said, "We'll take care of that." You yanked a new pair of overalls from the counter, told Mom to clean me up, and then said to me, "If you get in mud again, your bottom will be so sore you will not enjoy sitting for many days." I knew you meant it.

I went to school in the new overalls with much more confidence. I had overalls just like the other boys. What I did not realize was that most of them had never had a new pair of overalls. So my name was changed to "New Pants," and my status was the same.

I guess I was sort of dumb relative to the ways of life, and it took me some time to realize that I would be fighting every day unless I learned how to fight. I was small for my age, so I could see myself fighting forever. Maybe a little thinking was in order.

A fight would begin with each participant trying to land a "hay-maker" that would immediately eliminate the competition. Most of the time the "hay-makers" never landed, so the fight ended as a wrestling match. I reasoned, "I could never win at either of these." So I decided to try another approach. After a missed "hay-maker" my opponent would be a bit off-balance, so I would rush him, hug him, and start the wrestling match. However, as I rushed my opponent, I would try jabbing his nose with my left fist with the middle finger extended about a quarter of an inch.

After a few practices, I did cause some bloody noses and a few yellow eyes, when I missed the nose and hit the edge of the eye. Those choosing to fight me began to decrease. I thought it was because my one pair of overalls was beginning to show a bit of wear. More likely, it was because of complaints such as, "Buddy does not fight fair."

Thirteen years later in an army unit in which an eager lieutenant arranged all types of athletic competition between platoons, I easily won the lightweight boxing for my platoon. Someone asked, "Where did you learn to box?" I hesitated to say, "In my early years in school, I learned to fight to survive."

The next big change in my life occurred because of your dedication to education. Sis was just too smart. She was being promoted too often and soon would need the opportunity to attend high school. You asked a few of your merchandise salesmen to look for a general store for rent with possible living arrangements in the store similar to our present situation. The new store had to be in driving distance of a high school. Soon we were nailing pasteboard boxes on the walls and papering with newspapers in another side room in a store at Pig, Kentucky.

My living conditions were certainly helpful to a mischievous boy. There was no way, unless I was asleep, that I could keep from hearing your prayers each night. Always you were praying that I would learn to be a good boy. I hoped that later in life I would not disappoint you. I was not certain about right then.

You were avid supporters of learning at school. In fact, you pushed me constantly to do better work at my new school, Capitol Hill, a one room school with eight grades and one teacher. I was more interested in practical experience, and I did learn many practical lessons at this time. Remember my best pal, M.G. Sumpter, who lived on the farm across the street from the store. His dad had four big, white-faced steers. He also had hanging in the hallway of the barn two old wooden yokes, which had been used by his grandfather. One day M.G. and I were studying in school how the early settlers moved across the country with their wagons pulled by oxen. An idea was born. With the help of M.G.'s nephew and my cousin Ned, two big steers were hitched to a cart. Then we started our imaginary ride from coast to coast. M.G.'s nephew was supposed to walk by the side of the steers and guide them in a direction planned in advance. He stumbled and spooked the steers. They began running at top speed for nowhere.

"Whoa! Whoa!" yelled M.G, forgetting we were driving steers, not mules.

We were afraid to jump from the cart and afraid to stay in the cart.

"I want out!" Ned yelled, but we knew he could not get out without the possibility of a broken arm or something.

"They are headed for the mulberry tree, the one with the low branches! Put your head low and cover your eyes!" warned M.G.

"Ouch! Oh me! It hurts!" we yelled as the branches raked our bodies.

"Oh no! There's a small gully at the bottom of the hill," warned M.G. "Hold tight to anything you can find."

The cart bounced two feet in the air as we hit the gully, but it did not turn over.

"My bottom! My bottom!" Ned moaned.

"They are headed for the creek now," yelled M.G.

When we hit the creek, water went everywhere. We got wet. The steers stopped in the middle of a creek. I jumped out on one side, and M.G. on the other, and each of us grabbed a halter on a steer. Now creek water is really cold in Kentucky in January. We survived this "coast to coast" trip with only sore throats and runny noses. I learned from this escapade, "Never fool with animals, either two-legged or four-legged, that are smarter than you are."

I am certain you recall how much I enjoyed the outdoors. I really enjoyed "possum hunting." Usually, I went "possum hunting" with older boys, and this made me feel big. I knew where the big persimmon trees were located, and possums love persimmons. I guess I am kin to a possum because there is nothing better than a big orange persimmon after a couple of frosts.

One night I went hunting with two eighth graders, J.T. Skaggs and Gordon Wilson. The area where we hunted is now a part of Mammoth Cave National Park. We could hear the barking of old Rover way off in the distance. We ran like mad to get to him because good possum hides were selling for thirty cents, and we didn't want to give the possum a chance to jump out of the tree. We ran as fast as we could, but the barking still sounded far away. "I believe old Rover must be in Cedar Sink," J.T. called out breathlessly. "I hope not," Gordon gasped, and we all agreed.

Cedar Sink consisted of several acres of land that thousands of years ago just decided to sink about fifty feet. The land down at the bottom was very rich so farmers used a mule trail to get to the ground level of the sink, and then used a wire and pulley to lower a plow and later to pull up the corn. Since no one used Cedar Sink, except for summer farming, some said it was a haven for bears, bobcats, and other wild animals just waiting for a mouthful of a tender young boy.

When we finally got to the rim of Cedar Sink, J.T. whistled for Rover. All that could be heard was a muffled bark. Gordon tried his dog calling ability, "Here Rover! Here Rover!" Rover had no intention of leaving his night's work. "Let's just leave Rover here and go home," I suggested. "No way," said J.T. "My dad would kill me if I left him." Gordon argued, "You guys are stupid, if you think I'm going in there. I'm gonna find my way home." "Look," pleaded J.T. "I've got to get my dog. Are you my friends or not?" Soon we were on a trail, inching down the rim of Cedar Sink. Following the sound of his barks, we finally found Rover. He had located something in a trap back in a small cave. J.T. tried to entice him with a biscuit, but he would not leave his prize possession. Finally, we had to go down in the cave to get him.

Just as J.T. got hold of Rover's collar, the ferocious animal in the trap stood up. It was a beautiful black animal with a big white stripe down its back. It sprayed all three of us. Being sprayed by a skunk at close range was an unforgettable experience. When I got home, even though it was very cold, I removed all of my clothes outside and slipped into the house. About 3:00 a.m. my smell awakened you, Dad. You put a big bucket of water on the stove, gave me a washrag and a cake of lye soap with instructions, "Don't come back in this house until you smell better." The bath did not help much, but you finally allowed me back in the house because of the freezing weather.

None of us was popular at school the next day, but all were allowed to stay in school provided we would sit on the back row. I had buried my clothes six inches under the surface of the ground, and in about two weeks they were ready to be washed for future wear. Through life when I have had the inclination to meddle, I remember this encounter with a skunk, and my motto has been, "Don't meddle in other people's business. They might be in a trap."

Remember Dad when you said, "Buddy, I believe you would try anything once." Yes, I guess I was a reckless youngster, but I really enjoyed life. I was not certain about "schooling."

During the Great Depression it seemed that boys started dropping out of school in rural areas in about the fifth grade and continued to drop from school through high school. Some of them were needed on the farms to help make a living. Others liked to work at day labor in order to have a little spending money. A typical high school senior class at my school consisted of twenty girls and four boys. Mom and Dad, you thought you were doing a good job keeping me in school; however, I never told you, but the real reason I stayed in school is written on a piece of paper in one of the two cigar boxes.

You explained to me many times that the Great Depression was bad, and it was, but the worst was yet to come. Just as my generation was entering the carefree years of adolescence, the Japanese attacked Pearl Harbor, and thus pushed our country into World War II. Plans for any kind of a future for youngsters my age had to be postponed. To our work ethic we added patriotism, bravery, and sacrifice; and many gave their young lives. We dared not consider what could happen to us, but were forced to focus our attention on what needed to be done. All able- bodied young men were being drafted to meet the demands of World War II. The most difficult part was leaving behind your sweetheart, knowing you would see little of her for maybe three or four years. The one

I loved received an abundance of letters because two soldiers were in love with her. Which one, if either, would she marry? The answer to this question is also found in one of the old cigar boxes.

At a very early age you taught me to pray, to honor God, and to appreciate His goodness. You also taught me that God expected me to behave, but somehow I was always forgetting this admonition. We attended church regularly, so what happened to me at the revival being held in the old Cole School building by a Methodist evangelist should not have been a surprise. You felt that the family should attend the services, but we had closed the store so late that we had to sit on the back row. I had taken a good nap leaning against Dad, but was awakened by the shouting of the evangelist, "You sinner, back there on the back row, you're heading straight for hell. You're going to burn up in hell if you don't change your ways."

Now there was probably a sizeable group of sinners on the back row as that was usually where they sat after taking their last minute smoke or drink before coming inside. However, I was certain the evangelist was talking directly to me. "Did you hear me, sinner?" yelled the preacher. I thought, "How could I keep from hearing you?" The preacher continued, "God's telling you right now to turn from your wicked ways. Come on down to the mourner's bench and ask God to forgive your sins." I wanted to go down to the mourner's bench, but I knew you would stop me. In those days, it was thought that at nine years of age I was too young to make such decisions.

That night I did not sleep very much. I prayed as the evangelist had said, "Dear God, won't You forgive my sins." Then I started listing some of these sins: "Yes, I pulled my sister's hair. Yes, I did hide my sister's history paper. Yes, it was I who broke the dish. There's way too many sins to list. Dear God, won't You just forgive all of my sins. You know, Lord, I do not want to go to hell. I do not want to burn up. Please save me." On and on I wrestled with the Lord. Toward morning my prayers had been answered.

But I had a problem the next morning. The preacher had said one needed to get up from the mourner's bench and confess that Christ was his Savior. I interpreted this to mean you needed to tell someone about your experience. Now I could not tell you or Sis. You would not understand. You thought I was too young. I needed someone I could tell about what Jesus had done for me. Who would that be? Finally, I had the answer. "I will tell Ruth."

As you know, I did not have much to do with girls. In fact, I wondered why God did not make everyone boys. But Ruth was different. In fact, if Ruth had been a boy, she would have been my best pal. Too bad, she had to be a girl. Ruth lived way back on a dirt road, and her father brought her very early to the store on his way to work at the tobacco warehouse in Bowling Green. I got up early, too. So Ruth and I played jacks every morning until it was time to walk to school. However, we did not walk to school together. The boys went in one group and the girls in another.

Ruth tossed the ball and began picking up the jacks by twos. "Ruth," I asked, "Were you at the revival last night?"

"No, Dad had to get up too early this morning to go to work."

"Well, the preacher said that if we did not accept Jesus as Lord and Savior we were going to hell."

"He did?" Ruth asked looking up from her jacks.

"And you know what, I came home and prayed most of the night and accepted Jesus as my Lord and Savior."

"You did?" Ruth asked with a surprised look on her face.

"I sure did, but I can't tell anyone but you because they will say that I am too young."

"You are?" she repeated as she began her threes.

"You won't tell anybody, Ruth?"

"Cross my heart and hope to die," she answered.

That's what I liked about Ruth. She didn't bore you to death with a lot of words.

She was the first girl I had ever really liked, but I liked her as a boy. She was certainly a good jacks player. Too bad she was a girl.

I gave my heart to the Lord at nine years of age, but I really did not appreciate what a wonderful thing had happened to me until later in life. This is also described in one of the two cigar boxes.

Well Mom, well Dad, everything is packed, and I am ready for the last time to lock the front door of what was once our happy home. I have in my hands the two old cigar boxes. I want to make certain I do not lose them again. I wonder if you had any idea of how much sorrow, how much heartache, and how much happiness are represented by the contents of these old cigar boxes. Cold chills are running up and down my spine just thinking about what is in these boxes.

Now that I have completed my assignment for Mom, I just have to take a quick glance at the contents of these boxes. Immediately my mind is consumed with bits and pieces of wonderful nostalgia. I marvel at how the contents of these two boxes describe the history of ten years of my life. But now I have a problem. I know I must return to the little railroad town in the hills of Kentucky, where these memories began, to make certain my recollection of what happened in each situation is accurate. I must place the notes, the mementos just where they rested long ago.

It is said that one can never really go back, but I have to go back. From the moment I opened the first cigar box, my days have been haunted by flickering glimpses of the past. I must go back to relive the events that completely changed my life.

Things that happen in our youth often affect our lives more than we are willing to admit. I was a young teenager in this little town, and I fell in love with my next-door neighbor, Polly. I loved her so very much that without my realizing it she influenced my every action. Now, as I write these words, I am amazed at how many life decisions bear the imprint of Polly's perceptive suggestions, when we were so very young. By reliving the past perhaps I can understand how one little girl had so much influence on me, mapping the highway of my journey through life.

I Fail At Love But Pass in Baseball

I'm almost there. A strange mixture of both anticipation and apprehension assail me. Perhaps I don't really want to relive everything. I turn off Highway 31 onto Highway 259, and remember how many times I have gotten off a Greyhound bus at this intersection to walk a mile to my home. Often it is in the middle of the night, and many times it is raining.

My mind wanders back to the time my family once moved over this same road. Mom and Dad had saved enough money to invest in a larger store. They also had felt the need for living in a real house, not the side room of a store. Granny Sullivan was now living with us, so we needed more room. Since my sister was a junior in high school, space was needed for entertaining her friends. Perhaps it was an answer to our prayers. A store did become available in Rocky Hill, where my sister was already enrolled in high school.

As I top the last hill before entering the town, my eyes begin to fill with tears. There's the Baptist church and the Methodist church, each located on its own special hill. The

Baptist church had Sunday school and preaching every Sunday, and the Methodist church had services every other Sunday. Our family attended the Methodist church two Sundays a month and the Baptist church the other Sundays. However, I enrolled in Sunday school and a Sunday evening youth program at the Baptist church. My parents made certain I was present every Sunday. They had no difficulty getting me to attend the Baptist youth program because Polly was always there.

As I drive slowly along the one main street, I see Polly's house and then my house, less than twenty feet apart. Time has taken its toll. Both are in much need of repair, but they still look like home. I stop the car next to the broken sidewalk in front of Polly's house. My mind begins to play tricks on me. I see her clearly, sitting in the swing on her porch. I remember correctly – she is a cute freckle- faced twelve-year-old girl. "Polly, Polly," I yell. My voice cracks and I can say no more.

There in the corner of her yard and right next to mine is that old maple tree. I see the teen age two of us sitting on an old quilt under the maple tree. During the war years I sang to her "Don't sit under the maple tree with anyone else but me." I am forced to look away. My heart is racing much too fast. The concrete porch in front of my house has many cracks. Gone are the two big rocking chairs that were always there. Polly and I often rocked in these, keeping time to a new song we had learned.

I glance across the street, and there's just a vacant weed infested spot where our first Rocky Hill house had been, our very first real house. In fact, I even had a room of my own. There was gas for heating, and since electricity was available, we purchased a radio. Then I could listen to my favorite radio programs, Fibber McGee and Molly, Amos and Andy,

Henry Aldridge, and of course the broadcast of the St. Louis Cardinal's baseball games. We got our water from a cistern. There was no inside plumbing so baths were taken in a round galvanized tub, and it was necessary to make trips down the hill to the out-house, even on cold days. But we had come a long way. We really did live in a house instead of the side room of a store.

At that time Rocky Hill was a small railroad town with about one hundred and twenty people, twenty dogs, sixteen cats, five cows, and two goats. It was once a thriving town, but U.S. Highway 31 from Louisville to Nashville had missed the town, so some businesses had closed. The Louisville and Nashville trains stopped twice a day, dropping off and picking up passengers and mail.

I am getting too emotional. I evidently have forgotten the plans I had for this trip, plans I formulated so meticulously. All the notes, letters, and mementos in the two cigar boxes have been arranged in just the right order to facilitate reliving my life. My plan is that as I remove each item from a given box, Polly will appear in my mind exactly as it happened in life. This is necessary if I am to learn why she had so much influence on my life.

This thin copper colored oval object from the cigar box is a penny that I once placed on a railroad track to be flattened by the wheels of a freight train. It brings back happy memories. Railroad tracks and trains fascinate me. During my first few nights in Rocky Hill I cannot sleep because of the lonely train whistle. First there is a low mournful sound as a train approaches from a distance. Then the whistle gets louder and louder. It seems that the train shakes the whole town as it moves down the tracks at a high speed. The noise is terrible. However, in just a few weeks I learn to sleep right through it. I especially enjoy watching passenger trains. Often the windows are open and people are waving. I wonder who they are and where they are going.

One of our favorite pastimes is to see who can walk on the rails the longest distance without falling off. Most of my new friends in Rocky Hill can do much better than I, but I am learning quickly how to be a talented "rail walker." My friend, Paul Cramer, and I spend much time walking the rails in late afternoon, expounding on our undeveloped philosophies of life.

There is a long railroad siding in Rocky Hill, and freight trains pull in this siding to let other trains pass. We know, that once in a siding, a train must stop at some point so the switch can be turned to get out of the siding. So we feel safe climbing the steel ladder outside of a boxcar. Sometimes, we climb to the top for a short ride; other times we hold onto the steel ladder. We have plenty of time to jump off before the conductor can pull the switch to get back on the main line. We enjoy this pastime without the approval of our parents. One day Paul suggests, "Let's not wait for the train to stop. Let's swing up on the ladder while the train is moving." "Suits me," I reply as I start running, catch the steel bar of a ladder, jump in the air and start riding the boxcar. Paul follows on the next boxcar. From that time on we never get on or off a train while it is stopped. Our families would have been very unhappy if they had known what we were doing. I guess Dad was right when he once accused me of being a reckless youngster.

✧

I do not have enough time to explore all the new things in Rocky Hill, because my parents are always finding something to take the place of my fun. Although I am only eleven, my parents think I am old enough to help them in the store on Friday evenings and Saturdays. The top priority for my services is helping Dad with the produce. Produce is that which is purchased from the farmers, providing spending money for them. Produce consists mainly of hen eggs, live chickens, molasses, cured smoked ham, fresh meat, and cream. While Dad is weighing the items to be purchased from a farmer and serving him as a customer, I am carrying six squawking chickens (tied together at their legs) to the chicken house. Sometimes there is a cured ham to hang in the meat room.

Dad grins when he says I am in charge of "candling eggs." It's not all that bad since here is the process I use. A hole is cut in a pasteboard box. The hole is just smaller than most eggs. A 100-watt bulb is placed in the box underneath the hole. When holding an egg up to the hole, I can see inside the egg: sometimes a baby chick, sometimes the start of a baby chick, sometimes a big red glob, and sometimes just a red ring. Any one of these conditions means the egg is not fresh. I carefully lay aside the bad eggs for returning to the owner. Indeed I handle them very carefully, because a broken bad egg has a terrible smell. The thing that I hate most about candling eggs is the fact that in a big basket of eggs there is always one or two that are crushed. I hate sticky eggs.

This piece of pink ribbon is from one of Polly's dolls, which I kidnap for a few hours. She makes like she is not very happy with me, but I think she enjoys my teasing her. There is something different about this cute, freckle-faced girl who lives across the street from our house. Although I am not yet ready to admit that girls exist, this one has caught my attention in a way I cannot explain. One day during spring-cleaning time when my mother has me washing windows, I slyly glance at the girl on top of her porch roof washing the upstairs windows of her house. I think I see her glancing at me. Each of us has to be careful so the other will not see our glances. There is no warning that this exchange of glances might be the start of something big in my life.

As I rub my hand over an old worn out wooden peg, I realize this peg is very special. Dad believes that an idle boy is a boy that is going to get in trouble. Thus he makes plans for keeping me busy. Although I get no pay for working in the store, I am allowed to keep all of the money I earn working on the farms near Rocky Hill. After a rain, the farmers hire anybody they can find to help "set" their tobacco. Plants are pulled from a bed and dropped in a row, and a good "setter" will bend over and start "pegging" – making a hole with a wooden peg, putting the plant in the hole and firmly packing dirt around the plant then on to the next plant, and finally to the last plant in the row without straightening up. This is backbreaking work, but I certainly won't admit it. After about two rows there is a blister on my hand, so the position of the wooden peg is changed to make room for the next blister. By noon my hand is covered with blisters; then blisters are rubbed on blisters. But never mind, I am earning twenty-five cents an hour.

On hot July days, I clean out the weeds and grass between cornrows with a rake pulled by a stubborn mule. My pay is $1 a day. "Setting tobacco" is a gold mine in comparison to "knocking out weeds." I often work for a farmer who has a mule with a mind of his own. At the end of a row, if the mule is real hot, he heads for the shade. There is no way anyone can stop him. Before the summer is over, I am most appreciative of this mule, who knows when it is time to rest.

I cannot understand why thoughts of that cute little girl, Polly, continue to clutter my mind. I do enjoy being with her at the youth program at the Baptist church. She always has a big smile for me. Sometimes she plays the piano in church, as her dad leads the singing. The discovery that she is very talented, in addition to being cute, adds additional fuel to my feelings for her. One thing I do not like. She is always winning when competing against the smart boys in the arithmetic and spelling competition in school. I am very glad I am two years ahead of her in school so I don't have to compete with her.

Polly is at the store to purchase ten pounds of Irish potatoes, and I am the only clerk in the store. Teasing I say, "I'm sorry, we don't have any Irish potatoes."

"You don't?"

"No but we have some Idaho potatoes."

The men loafing in the store giggle and laugh. Polly blushes so much that I can hardly see her freckles as she replies, "That will do."

I am surprised she is even prettier when she is blushing. I'll have to find ways to make her blush more often. Why is it that to me she is the cutest thing in the world?

I recognize an old red shipping tag as a part of a happy period in my life. The summer before we move to Rocky Hill I make a name for myself picking strawberries. Another strawberry season is rapidly approaching. Rocky Hill is seven miles from the patch. I will be too tired to be a great picker after walking the seven miles. I have an idea, one that will help win favor with Polly. I approach Dad with a business deal. I will take from my hard-earned bank account enough money to purchase one-half the cost of a bicycle. Then I will ride the bike the seven miles to pick strawberries. As I am paid weekly, I will reimburse him for the remaining cost of the bicycle. News is circulating by word-of-mouth that they are paying twenty-five cents a crate for picking strawberries this year. In no time the bicycle will be mine. Dad is not in favor of this deal because it teaches me "bad business practices." You do not purchase anything until you have enough money to pay for it. On the other hand, he hesitates to ask me to walk seven miles before working. He agonizes over this decision for some time. Finally, I purchase my bicycle. This is a great event in my life. I watch for the opportune time, and one day I see Polly sitting on the porch swing all by herself. I ride my new bicycle down the sidewalk and stop in front of her house. "Want to ride my new bike?"

"It's very pretty."

I have to brag a little. "I purchased it with money I made picking strawberries."

"You did? It sure is a nice one."

"Want to ride it."

"I might have a wreck and scratch it. I'm just learning to ride."

"Don't worry about that. I'm a reckless rider and will have lots of wrecks."

She bravely straddles my bicycle and rides down the street. I say to myself, "She can ride my bike any time she wants to." Polly rides up and down the street three or four times. Each time she gets ready to stop I wave her on. When she finally stops, I notice she is sweating, her face is flushed, and her freckles are cuter than ever.

"I really like your bike. Thanks for letting me ride."

"You can ride it any time you want." As I ride down the street, I am smiling. I hope this is the beginning of a long period of sharing my bike with Polly.

A note on a small scrap of paper reminds me, "Dad is real sick today." He is sick, and the country doctors cannot determine the cause. After many months of illness, they finally decide he has diabetes, but the prescribed medicine is not effective. He improves little until insulin comes to our "neck of the woods," and then his health improves immediately.

Dad's illness adds new work responsibilities to my already complicated life. Before school, I am supposed to help open the store, which involves building a fire in the big coal stove, making certain the supply of coal will last the entire day, and then sweeping the store. The store is hard to sweep since the floor has not been oiled for some time. About twice a year we

oil the floor of the store to control the dust. To oil the floor
we cover it with a thin coat of something that looks like mo-
tor oil.

After I clean the store, I assume the responsibility of serving customers so Mother can prepare breakfast before time
for me to go to school. My most interesting job is fixing my
own lunch, making certain I have plenty of candy kisses to
share with friends at school, especially Polly.

Late in the day I assume responsibility for the store so
Mother can cook the evening meal. Then I am supposed to
study. I often have other activities in mind other than study.
In Dad's absence, I am always back in the store before closing
time to help Mother lock the store.

Secretly, I have had my eye on Polly for some time, but I
am too bashful to say much to her. To get her attention I do
steal her book and take it for a bicycle ride, and when there
are no boys around to tease me, I share bicycle rides with her.
Occasionally a group of us practice our rail walking down
below the depot. It is something at school that causes me to
forget my inhibitions. The senior class is producing the play
Aunt Samantha Rules the Roost, which involves two students
who are not seniors. One plays the part of a young house-
maid, and the other plays the part of a grocery delivery boy.
Polly and I are selected for these two parts. The plot of this
humorous play is that the women purchase "love powders,"
which are supposed to improve the romantic interests of their
boyfriends. I am overjoyed that I am playing the part of Polly's
boyfriend.

Of course, Polly and I are not playing the lead parts in the play, so there is ample time for talking between scenes. My pockets are always filled with candy kisses. I know the way to this girl's heart. I really enjoy teasing Polly, making her blush, and watching her freckles disappear. She is the prettiest girl in the whole world. Is something terrible happening to me? Am I falling in love with Polly? This is my first experience with this sort of thing, and I do not know what to do about it.

Our small high school at Rocky Hill still has chapel programs once a week. Usually there is a short devotional followed by a student program. The remainder of the period is devoted to announcements. Principal Watson is loaded with announcements for this Friday. Last of all he begins talking about the senior play. "You certainly want to advertise the senior play to all of your friends. You won't want to miss this great production yourself because of the following human-interest story. All of you know Polly, who is in the eighth grade, and Buddy who plays second base on our baseball team."

He pauses with everybody turning to look at Polly who is sitting close to the front on the right side, and then looking at me. I am occupying my favorite spot on the back row. Polly begins turning white, and then pink, but nothing like she will turn in another fifty seconds. I drop my head, looking for a way to slip out the back door. Principal Watson continues, "In the play, Polly feeds Buddy love powders which are supposed to make him very romantic. In rehearsal we have been using sugar instead of the love powders, which we are saving until the night of the performance. However, Buddy evidently does not know this because during the rehearsal yesterday afternoon, he was seen behind the curtain kissing Polly's hand."

The students shout, they laugh, they yell, they clap their hands, but worse than this they look at Polly and then at me, and neither of us can find a hole in which to crawl. The principal closes the chapel period with, "You won't want to miss this performance; there is no telling what Buddy will do when he gets the real love powders."

The performance goes well because Polly is a born performer, and somehow I manage to remember the right words although I do the whole performance looking at the floor. The rest of the year I stay on the baseball field as much as possible. There are no girls there. I keep asking myself the question, "How can this love business happen to me?"

Yes, baseball will replace girls for me. Dad, who is a big man weighing two hundred and thirty pounds, is my inspiration. He tells that he was quite a baseball player when he was young. I enjoy listening to him talk about his baseball accomplishments. My number one goal in life is to make Dad proud of my baseball playing. I have really worked hard to make the high school baseball team as a sophomore. All of the baseball uniforms are much too big for me, but I put rubber bands here and there and scatter twenty or thirty safety pins so the uniform will not fall off. My sis says I look much like a clown in a circus.

The Friday afternoon game with Sunfish High is a real loser for me. Dad is sick most of night before the game and cannot attend to see me play. Then the older boys on the team indicate it is time for me to grow up and chew tobacco with the rest of them. You are not a man in Rocky Hill until you can spit tobacco juice at least six feet and hit a twelve-inch target.

Feeling sorry for myself because Dad is not at the game, I decide the time has come, so I start the game with a wad of "Apple Sweet" in my jaw. I hit home plate with tobacco juice several times and have other near misses. Everything is going well until a hard grounder is hit between first and second bases. I finally get to the ball, scoop it up, and throw out the runner at first. I hear the coach yell, "Great play."

I am really feeling good. This is the ideal time to give second base another splatter. I give a big spit, but the liquid is perfectly clear. "Holy Smoke! What has happened to my chew?" I return to where I caught the grounder – no chew of tobacco there. "Do you suppose when I reached to pick up the fast grounder that I could have swallowed my tobacco?" The answer to this question comes quickly.

In my next turn at bat, I am so sick I can barely make it to the plate. "Strike one," the umpire yells, but I have not seen the ball. I reason I cannot stand at the plate and let the umpire call three strikes. I must swing whether I can see the ball or not. The pitcher does a big wind-up, and I give a big swing on a pitch that hits the dirt at least a foot in front of the plate. "The pitcher will do better next time." But I am wrong. "Strike three," the umpire yells, as I swing on a pitch evidently a foot above the strike zone.

The coach has some choice words for me upon returning to the bench. He just cannot understand how his player who has such a sharp eye can swing at two bad pitches. It is even worse the next inning. I make two errors and when the inning is over, I notice the coach is striking my name from the line-up. I ask, "Can I go to the toilet, coach? I do not feel good."

The one-seater I occupy will never have another visitor like me. Words are not available to describe my sickness. In addition, I turn a dark green color, much like a big bullfrog.

At the next practice the coach says, "If you are going to chew tobacco during the game, Buddy, you must chew at every practice so you will learn not to swallow it." The older players told the coach what had happened to me.

The next summer is the greatest summer of my life. Sis is home from college; Polly is lonely; she visits with Sis at some time just about every day. For this reason I do not work on neighboring farms as much as usual. Instead I am happy to work in the store. When I am not serving a customer, I stay near the front windows of the store. From this position I can easily see Polly crossing the street. As soon as I can get away, I fill my pockets with candy kisses or something else good to eat and drop by the house. It is wonderful just sitting, talking, and looking at Polly for a few minutes. I really have a bad case of puppy love, and I have no idea what to do about it.

Love Is Not Easy

The best laid plans of mice and men sometimes go astray. Mom and Dad moved to Rocky Hill so my sister could finish her last two years of high school, and I would be able to attend high school if I should decide to start studying. Much to their surprise, I have completed two years of high school. Thank goodness, because now we have the official proclamation that the Rocky Hill High School is too small to operate economically so the high school will be closed. However, a school bus will be provided to transport the Rocky Hill students eleven miles to Brownsville High School.

Occasionally someone remembers the "hand-kissing" story, but most of the time the teasing on the bus is about something else. I soon have the reputation of being the leader of the Terrible Termites, who are known for their vicious teasing. This is an outgrowth of being in love and not knowing what to do about it. I have heard people talk about puppy love, and I assume this is what has happened to me. From what I hear, puppy love is not mature, will not last, and will disappear with time. But sometimes puppy love is the real thing, lasting forever. What I need to know is how can I tell whether my love is the lasting kind or the kind that will disappear. I long for an answer. Since I have no answer, it seems my only solution is to seek a happy-go-lucky, carefree life with the belief this will cause puppy love to disappear.

Polly begins immediately to make a name for herself academically at her new school. On every test, hers is the highest score. Even as a freshman, she becomes the star pupil at Brownsville High School. I can do well in my classes when I try, but my goal is to excel athletically, even though I have not been endowed with great ability in this direction. I play as a substitute on the basketball team. However, my first love is baseball, and I play two years on the team that is described by a Louisville sports writer as the miracle team in Kentucky. In spite of the hours spend at basketball and baseball practice, my grades seem to improve because of my love for Polly. Instead of B's and C's, my report card now contains A's and B's. My concern that a brilliant girl like Polly might not have an interest in a lazy student works wonders for me. Love is truly a powerful encourager.

Dad expects me now, as a fourteen-year-old teenager, to increase my share of work in the store. He begins to visualize that maybe one day I will be his partner in operating a general store. Therefore he must teach me honesty and integrity. He lectures, "Buddy, we have three hundred-pound bags of sugar to put into ten pound bags. Make certain each bag weights a bit over ten pounds, as we always want to give honest weight."

I am just about organized and ready to start, and there is Dad again with additional instructions. "Remember you cannot get ten ten-pound bags of sugar from one hundred pounds. Regardless of how careful you are, one bag will weigh slightly more than ten pounds. This means to get ten bags, one bag will have to weigh less than ten pounds. We don't want to cheat anyone." Then he concludes with, "To be known as a man of honesty and integrity is much more important in life than being a rich man. You can lose your money, but a good name will last forever."

Sometimes I feel Dad carries honesty to the extreme. Some people take advantage of his honesty. A customer complains, "Mr. Baskins, Buddy made a dollar mistake when giving me change yesterday." I am certain no such mistake has been made. Nevertheless, the cash register rings, and the customer receives a dollar. Dad practices the axiom that the customer is always right.

While Dad is seriously ill with diabetes, I become the driver of the family car. At fourteen with no driving experience, except I know how to start and stop, I fear for what might happen to the car. It has rained all morning, and ice has frozen on the road all afternoon. During the night it snows on top of the ice. It nearly knocks me over when I am told Dad must have some medicine from a neighboring town. Although I am scared, there is no choice. With a few basic instructions I am on my way. Dad's final words are, "Remember, drive slowly and always cut toward the way you are sliding. Do not apply the brakes. This will cause you to slide sideways."

Everything is going well until the car approaches a ninety-degree turn just before entering the town. The car is going downhill and gaining speed. I do not believe it can make the ninety-degree turn. I visualize the car in the ditch. How can I get it out? In spite of Dad's admonition I just have to touch the brakes. Immediately the car spins round and round, and when it stops it is headed in the wrong direction. My heart is beating much too fast. I pray what is probably the most sincere prayer of my life, "Thank you Lord for watching over my driving." I then calmly turn the car around and head into the town to get the medicine.

When I am working in the store by myself, there are usually many loafers, older men who are at the store not as customers but to sit around the pot-bellied stove and exchange tales. They joke and laugh with me and become my very good friends. Actually some of them are at the store when I am by myself in order to protect me if someone should cause me difficulty. Shorty Moore, living in a one room house below my garden, is one of these loafers. Shorty is always good to me, giving me fruit and grapes from his orchard. As I am working in my garden I see Shorty coming up the hill toward me. As his short legs scurry up the hill, he reminds me of a circus clown, round in all directions and a nose that is always red. Then I see his face is scarlet red, which means he is drinking too much or is angry. Today both are true.

"Where were you at 8:30 last night?" he asks belligerently.

"I worked in the store until 9:00."

"Good," he replies with a frown on his face.

"Why is that?"

"I would have shot a bunch of boys last night except I thought you might be in the group. That bunch of scoundrels need to be taught a lesson."

"How come?"

"First they shake all the ripe apples from my tree. Then when I chase them away, they throw rocks on the tin roof of my house. If they ever do that again, I'm going to spray them with buckshot."

"But you might hit someone in the eye."

"I don't care. They are a bunch of animals. Come see the big dents the rocks made in my roof."

When I see three of the guys that I think were in the group-disturbing Shorty, I really do not know a good way to introduce the subject, so I blurt out, "You should not tease old Shorty so hard. He gets real excited, and could have a heart attack."

"Who cares?" they reply.

"But he is an old man."

"And a mean old man, at that! You should have heard how he cursed us when we got a few apples."

"Then you damaged his roof with rocks."

"Quit trying to defend that old goat! We know you are his pet."

"I'm not trying to defend him. I'm trying to help you as a friend. Sometime he is going to shoot you with buckshot. He could hurt you."

"Tell the old goat to stay out of our way or he will get hurt."

Sometimes there is simply no way to win.

There is no bank in Rocky Hill, so Baskins General Store does banking business in Brownsville, where I go to high school. On banking days I drive the car to school. At lunch I take a sack full of checks to be deposited, and the banker fills the sack with bills and change for the operation of the store.

The car is securely locked until after school. One morning Dad instructs, "Tell the banker he made a mistake of $32 in my favor. Here is my check to cover it." When I present the $32 check, the banker says, "Buddy, your dad is probably right. He usually is. At the end of the week, when we balance the books we can tell whether we keep the check or return it to him." Then, the banker makes a statement that makes me proud. "You should really admire your dad. He is known as one of the most honest men in this county." This day I will never forget.

Maybe someday people will say that I am an honest man. I should be because my family insists that I be at church four times each Sunday: Sunday school, morning worship service, youth program, and evening worship service. About this time a revival is in progress at the Rocky Hill Baptist Church. According to local belief, I am old enough now to join the church. Everybody is expecting me to be saved during this revival. In fact, Polly has made a couple of talks at our youth program about being saved, and I feel she is directing them at me. There is one problem. I do not feel lost. I gave my heart to the Lord when I lived at Pig, and there is no question in my mind that I am bound for heaven. But how to handle this delicate situation poses a problem for me.

I could join the church and say I was saved many years ago, but that introduces the problem of explaining the circumstances. I could go forward for rededication, but that also demands explanation. I decide to go forward and announce I have been saved and want to join the church. Thankfully the preacher does not ask when it happened so no explanation is necessary. Some people wonder why I am joining Polly's church and not the church of my family. But then they do not know I am in love with Polly.

✧

An old clipping from the state paper, the Courier Journal, is just what I need to make me smile. Everyone needs to find his name in a state paper once in lifetime. I am not making much progress in this love thing, but baseball is another story. Brownsville High School is very small, even after the transfer of students from Rocky Hill. However, our baseball team has two very good pitchers, and this is enough to carry our team through district and regional competition and into the final eight of state competition two years in a row. I lose my favorite spot at second base, but the coach explains, "I have never seen anyone who can determine as well as Buddy where a fly ball is going immediately after it leaves the bat." Yes sir, I can really snag a fly in that outfield.

In 1940 Brownsville High School easily wins all games in district and then regional competition and heads for the Kentucky state tournament. Since our high school is so small in enrollment in comparison to the other schools in this tournament, the state sports writers have a lot to say about "poor little Brownsville High."

We catch their attention when we easily win the first game of the tournament. When we defeat the largest high school in Louisville for the second game, everyone is pulling for the "miracle team" to win the tournament. Oh, for one more pitcher! Because we have only two good pitchers, we are not even competitive in the final game.

In 1941, Brownsville High has the same problem. We win the first two games of the tournament but lose the final game. However, I come home from the tournament with some good memories. My batting average is over .400 in the tournament, and I snag some good catches that receive applause. My biggest thrill comes in the second game when I am a part of two rallies that win the game. In the back of my mind there is the thought, "I bet Polly will be proud of me now." The following article appears in the Louisville Courier Journal.

Brownsville, Manuel Move to Finals in Diamond Meet

Brownsville staged a storybook finish in its game with Ashland to advance to the finals of the state high school baseball tournament along with duPont Manuel of Louisville.

Ashland started out as if it intended to have an easy time with Brownsville and went into the last inning sporting a 4 – 0 lead. Brownsville had made only four hits up to that time. Goodsen, a 13-year-old eighth grader was sent in as a pinch hitter to start the story book seventh inning, and the little southpaw, who is hardly taller than the big bat he carried to home plate, promptly dropped a Texas league single into left. Baskins, Dunlap, Sumpter, and Barlow followed with singles, and a fielder's choice on a ball hit in the infield allowed the final run to score, sending the game into extra innings.

Washington, the winning pitcher, allowed Ashland one run in the eighth, and again it seemed that Ashland was going to win. Young Goodsen, second up in the eighth inning, got his second single into left field. Baskins singled, Dunlap struck out, and Sumpter rapped a double into right-center for the winning tally.

A friend sends me what he heard over the radio. This account is far more interesting to me than the newspaper article:

Well, we are right back where we were in the seventh when this Brownsville team scored four runs and took the game into extra innings. Ashland is ahead by one run, there is one out, and we start with the same group that performed the miracle in the seventh. Here we go! Young Goodsen gets his second single. Are we starting a second comeback?

Baskins is at the plate. The Ashland fans are really giving him the razzle-dazzle. He has played a great game, robbing Ashland of a couple of good hits with his sensational catches. He is a cool one. To show his contempt for the Ashland fans, he spits tobacco juice all over home plate. He always fakes a bunt on the first pitch, hoping to bring the infield in close so he can get a hit. The pitcher is doing a good job, one ball, and two strikes. Don't give him a decent pitch are the instructions from the bench. The next pitch is a high roundhouse curve that is going way outside. Baskins reaches across the plate and drops his second single over the first baseman's head. There's no question that Baskins likes high outside pitches.

Dunlap strikes out. The ball game is one out from being over. Sumpter is at bat. He gets a good hit in short right field. Goodsen is going to score, and the game is tied again. Wait a minute! Wait a minute! Baskins is not slowing down at third. The coach is sending him in. He can't possibly get all the way from first to home plate on that hit. Look at that jackrabbit run. The Ashland catcher is blocking the plate. Baskins does a perfect slide around him. The game is over. The team with the heart won this game.

I am a success on the baseball field, but a romantic hero I am not. My excuse is the extremely difficult circumstances that prevail. There's no question that I have a bad case of puppy love for Polly. By this time my feelings for her are even more special, but I have little opportunity to let her know of my feelings, even though her house is across the street from mine.

Polly is an only child and lives in a protective environment. Her father is a big man, tall and muscular. When Charley Payne is in his Kentucky Highway Patrol uniform with his pistol attached to his belt, he is a formidable obstacle to a fifteen-year-old youngster. He is not a preacher, but is known as Mr. Baptist Church by all who know him. He unlocks the Baptist church and closes it after the services. He is director of the Sunday school program, leads in singing at all worship services, leads in prayer meeting on Wednesday evenings, and has been head deacon for as long as anyone can remember. He is the church rock in Rocky Hill, very conservative, and not approving many things that young people enjoy.

Polly's mother is a talented elementary school teacher, loved by both students and parents. She is fifteen years younger than Charley. Permission for the extra things in life that Polly is allowed to enjoy is secured from Mr. Payne by Polly's mother. For example, attending movies is not on the approved list of things for Polly to do. She has seen only one movie when she graduates from high school, whereas movies are the fad for most of us as teenagers at this time. It takes courage for me to sit on the porch with Polly. Instead, I stop my bicycle on the sidewalk next to the hedge at the front of her house and talk to Polly in the swing on her porch for a few minutes before riding on down the street.

My biggest obstacle is that I am two years and one month older than Polly. If Mr. Payne should find out how I feel about his daughter, he would make it clear that a boy who is junior in high school has no business even looking at a thirteen-year-old freshman girl. It just is not done in his rulebook.

My only recourse is the church youth program on Sunday night. Of course, most of the time we have prepared programs, but no one can control an occasional smile, as you look across the room at a special someone. I am there every Sunday night.

The announcement in chapel at Rocky Hill about my puppy love for Polly should have taught me a lesson, but a teenage guy does not always use good judgment in matters of romance. During our first year at Brownsville High, I write notes to Polly in school and pass them to her in an algebra book. Then comes the catastrophe! One day I am confronted by a gang of so-called friends who have some of the notes. I can take the teasing, but my heart is broken because according to them Polly gave them the notes. Previously, I accused Polly of smiling a lot at one of my classmates, Tom Dunlap. Did this irritate her to the extent that she made the notes available to them to hurt me? If so, she accomplished her goal. One of the notes is given to her father, and I am not sure I should even attend Sunday night youth meetings any more. My admiration for Polly in my last year in high school is from afar. Although I still care for her, I am bitter at the same time.

At fifteen, Polly is more lovely than ever. Because of her outgoing personality, she is liked by all. The freckles are disappearing, and it is obvious to the teenage boys that she has a very nice figure. In fact, other fellows are looking her way, especially Tom Dunlap. She seems to think of me as a big tease who is determined to make life miserable for her. In no way will I ever let her know my true feelings toward her. In fact, I date her best friend several times and sit with her many days on the school bus simply hoping it will irritate Polly. In spite of anything I can do, my feelings for Polly continue to affect my life. I still go to youth programs every Sunday night just to be near her. I aim for goals that might impress her. For example, I study so hard that my graduating class votes me "most likely to succeed in life." This pleases my parents very much; they have no idea I have done this studying to impress Polly.

No matter how careful I am, my feelings for Polly sometimes surface unexpectedly. An air force training plane crashes near our high school. I am one of the first to get to the crash. We try to pull the pilot from the cockpit, but the plane is beginning to burn and the heat is unbearable. The smell of burning flesh and the expression on the burning face of the pilot are almost more than I can handle. Because of the heat, it is impossible to get him out of the plane. He dies before additional help arrives.

In the midst of this horror, I see Polly and some other girls rushing up the hill toward the accident. I run to meet Polly. I am really a mess. I have burns on my hand from the metal on the pilot's straps. I do not have on a shirt. My face and stomach are black from the grease of the plane. Sweat is running down through the grease. "Polly, don't go up there. It is terrible." She must have sensed the urgency in my voice because she stops in her tracks and runs back toward the school.

Receiving a senior class ring is a great event in my life since there were many temptations to drop out along the way. I proudly show it to Polly in Tom's presence on the school bus. Tom is my age , but he has two more years of high school. Maybe this will cause Polly to think a little.

As I finish high school, I realize my parents have been very good to me in my two years at Brownsville High School. On any day there is a baseball game, I am allowed to drive the car to school so I can stay after the school bus departs. In basketball season, I drive the car to school so I will have transportation to get home at night. Usually there is a carload of boys and girls from Rocky Hill who will stay for the ball games and ride home with me. Polly is never in this group. She is not allowed to ride in a car filled with youngsters. I so want her to see me make one of my fabulous catches in the outfield, but Mr. Payne can never arrange to bring her to a baseball game.

A school bus unloads the players at the high school for out-of-town games. Tom Dunlap is one of the players who rides with me to his home along the route to Rocky Hill. Tom is so jealous of me it is difficult for us to be friends, even though we have been classmates since grade school days. He must have some idea of my feelings for Polly.

I Try To Bargain With The Lord

I finish high school in May, 1941, and leave home in the middle of June for the big city of Nashville, Tennessee. I believe, at seventeen, I should be allowed to make my own decisions. This will not happen if I remain at home. Dad and I are bound to clash. We are too much alike.

My sister is graduating from college at age nineteen and will be teaching in high school and staying at home next year. I love my sister very much, but one more person in the decision-making process in my life is just too much.

However, my main reason for leaving home is that I must get away from Polly. I simply do not know how to deal with my feelings for someone I love, someone who is the most brilliant, talented girl I have ever known, someone I keep on a pedestal as my ideal Christian, someone who lives across the street, someone I see every Sunday night at the church youth program, and someone who is in and out of my house talking with my sister many times a day, but someone who considers me only as a good friend.

I have saved some money, Dad adds what is needed, and I purchase a one-year business course at Andrew Jackson University in Nashville, Tennessee. Mom is worried about my being in such a big city, so she undoubtedly gives Dad specific instructions to find a safe place for me to live. He does a good job. He finds a room at the Preston Boarding House. Except for my roommate, Randall Crew, also a student at Andrew Jackson University, all the other boarders are professional workers at the Baptist Sunday School Board. Many of the discussions at the dinner table concern articles they are writing, and it seems to me that most of the meals are simply mini- Sunday school classes. Maybe I need this.

Sis arrives home from college just in time to arrange a farewell party for me. Most of those invited are in my church youth group. The only thing different about this party and a typical church youth party is Polly. In previous weeks she has seemed very distant and aloof in her contacts with me. Maybe it is because I have teased her too much about her friend, Tom Dunlap. But on this occasion, she is the life of the party. I assume it is for one of two reasons: Either she really is sad to see me leave and is trying to make my last night at home a big success, or she is so happy to see me leave she can't control her happiness. It probably is the latter.

I do take advantage of the situation. In a game of passing from boy to a girl a ring on a toothpick held between the teeth, I whisper between my teeth to Polly, "Move your toothpick over to the right." She immediately cooperates. Then I move my toothpick to the other side. Of course, we do not pass the ring, but our lips touch for an instant. I get so excited that I drop the ring, and everybody is laughing including Polly. She is having a great time.

After the party my sister starts her usual questioning. "I thought you were supposed to have a date tonight."

"You can't spend time with dates at farewell parties; you have to be friendly with everyone."

"You talked more to Polly than you talked to your date."

"I didn't notice."

"I think you like Polly very much," she insists.

"It is just your imagination. In fact, she has a steady."

"I think Polly likes you."

"Now you are completely crazy."

The conversation ends as I stalk off to my bedroom.

In my first week in Nashville, I write letters to two boys and a letter to Polly. I simply can't cut all ties with Polly at this time. What if my love for her is the lasting kind?

1504 Linden Avenue, Nashville, June 16, 1941.
How is everything around Rocky Hill? I am sure things are improving now that the number one pest is out of town. I'm talking about the one who delights in teasing and aggravating you. I know I am a terrible tease, but I do not mean any harm. I hope you are not mad at me for my teasing Saturday night at the party. I want to leave home with as many friends as possible.

Buddy

Much to my surprise, Polly answers my letter. As a fifteen-year-old in Rocky Hill with little to do in the summer, perhaps she is lonesome. Her reply is in the form of a newspaper.

Rocky Hill News
Small Town Youngster Tries To Make Good
Leaving a wide gap of loneliness (and unaccustomed peace and quiet) in the town of Rocky Hill, which has seen him develop into a young man of great opportunity,

Buddy Baskins has gone forth to a new field, the field of higher education. His friends back home are proud of him and will expect him to return to them much better fitted for the full life ahead. The editor-ess herself wishes to give a figurative "pat – on – the – back" and say, "Go to it. I'm for you."

(The second article has the title, FFA Picnic Postponed, and the third article is Record Attendance at Annual Singing Convention. I move rapidly through these two articles because I know Tom was in attendance on both of these occasions and was probably holding hands with Polly, if Mr. Payne was not close-by. However, the last article really catches my eye.)

Personal Editorial

Speaking of teasing, I'd like to explain something. I hate to make unpleasant references, but I would like for you to know that I did not give those letters (remember) to the boys a year ago last fall. I read them hurriedly and wadded them up and stuck them way back in my desk to read later. I thought my desk was private, but I'm living to learn I suppose. If you remember, you wrote the last letter, and it was almost insulting. You called me deceitful, etc. It hurt, but I thought I understood how you felt so I skipped it just as I want you to skip this after you've read it. Forget it, please. This has been somewhere in my mind ever since that happened.

Eighteen months is a long time to wait to explain a situation. I suppose it is better now than never. Things might have been different if she had explained immediately.

✧

This newspaper from Polly does provide a great opportunity for a reply.

> This is the first paper I have received from this editor for two years. I am glad to receive it. I used to subscribe to this paper, but due to certain actions I have not received this paper for many months.
>
> As for the personal editorial, I really enjoyed it. I have been expecting such an editorial every day since October 28, 1939. This was the day I turned as white as this sheet of paper. My only knowledge is that the person who got the letters said it seemed to him that you placed them a certain place for him. I thought you might have made the letters available to him in order to hurt me. Since you never gave me an explanation, I tried not to think about the matter. However, down deep in my heart there has been a little hurt streak, which I hope no longer exists.

A catastrophe hits our family on July 4, 1941, less than a month after I leave home. A fire starts in the post office in the middle of the night. It spreads rapidly to two other adjoining small buildings, and then to the two-story drug store. The wind starts blowing toward our store across the street; the front of the store begins to burn. In a short time our house next door begins to burn. There is no fire department in Rocky Hill.

Some men explain to Dad, "We cannot fight the fire on your property by throwing water." (There was no water system in the town. Water came from cisterns and wells.) "The only way to save the rest of the town is to dynamite to the ground your home and store." Without a moment's hesitation Dad replies, "Go ahead." So the Baskins family loses just about everything because the house and store are dynamited before much can be removed. Dad is heard to say, "The Lord giveth, and the Lord taketh away."

I go home the next weekend to see about my family. As expected, they are doing well in spite of the calamity. As I walk by the charred remains of our store, I remember the many hours I have worked buying produce and selling merchandise. Never again will I candle an egg or drop a frying chicken through the trap door to the chicken house under the side room. Then I remember my many friends who were my special customers. To think that I will never relate to them again in this way haunts me. My plans do not include returning to Rocky Hill to make a living, but I am not ready for this break to come in such a rapid fashion.

As I walk to church on Sunday morning, Polly appears in the door of her house, and we walk to church together. She gives me her description of the fire, and offers her condolence. "Oh Buddy! It was terrible. I'm so sorry!"

"Did it scare you?" I ask.

"I haven't had a good night's sleep since the fire. I thought the whole town was going to burn. You should have seen how high the flames were going."

"I wish my family could have gotten more out of the house."

"It was terrible they had to dynamite the house so soon. I kept thinking if you were here you would have known what to do and how to get things out of the house."

"Sis lost all of her clothes."

"I told her she could borrow some of mine."

"How about me? I lost all of my winter clothes. Can I borrow some of your clothes?"

"You want to get kicked out of Nashville?"

"I bet I would look good in your clothes. By the way, I forbid you to ever ride my bicycle again."

"What?" Polly asks as she looks at me with a frown.

"Have you not seen its burned and warped frame in the ashes of the house?"

"Oh no!"

"We had some good times on that old bike. Didn't we?"

"You were always so kind to share your bike with me. We did have some good times together."

"When were you scared the most?" I ask.

"When your house started to burn, I got so scared I started carrying my things downstairs."

"All of those things that are dear to your heart?"

"Yes, all of those things I treasure and want to keep."

"Does that include my old letters?"

"Oh Buddy, you joke about everything."

We must have walked too rapidly. We are already at church. I am just getting warmed up for a great conversation with Polly. We do not sit together at church because Polly is the church pianist. At least, this is my excuse.

In the first letter I write home after the fire I inform my family of my intentions. I do a lot of thinking as I return to Nashville. I decide, in all fairness to my family, now is the time for me to begin supporting myself. I still have a few dollars in my bank account, and this will provide for room and board for some time. However, the following advertisement on the bulletin board at school catches my eye: "*Student wanted to do house and yard work for room and board.*" I make a telephone call, a visit, and immediately become a cook, dishwasher, house cleaner, and yard boy for an elderly lady.

This is a turning point in my life. At no time after this day do I ask my parents for financial help. I either find a way to earn what I need, or I do without. I am certain they would have sacrificed to help me, but I am too proud to be a burden. I talk to myself about Dad, "Old man, you made me assume responsibility at a very early age. Now the real thing has arrived. It will be interesting to see if I can handle it."

I can't get Polly out of my mind, so I search for ways to discourage her relationship with Tom. However, I always seem to fail.

The junior year of high school seems to be an exceedingly happy year for Polly. I guess that it is because I am not around to generate teasing. Academically, she is still the outstanding student at Brownsville High School. In addition, her steady boyfriend is the catch of the school. Not only is Tom the star basketball player of the school, he is handsome with black hair and dark eyes. He is crazy about Polly. They are together constantly. Polly saves him a seat on the school bus, and he carries her books and walks her to her classrooms. Tom has become an integral part of her life.

However, I keep writing Polly as if nothing is happening in our lives. We are both stubborn and neither will write until we receive a letter from the other. Sometimes I become so desperate I bury my pride and write when I have not received a letter from her. However, I try to find a logical excuse for such action. One day I notice an interesting article in a Nashville newspaper about Chinese love powders. This seems like a good excuse to write Polly.

I have enclosed a clipping I cut from a newspaper. It reminds me of an event that took place in my life. It may have been so long ago that you have forgotten. Just like Wong in the clipping, I was once given love powders. Wong became so softhearted that he did not prosecute his case in court. The love powders I was given by a cute little eighth grade girl with freckles seemed to get me in a lot of trouble. I apologize for cluttering your mind with this old memory.

I even try to find ways to cause trouble between Polly and Tom. This is difficult as I am in Nashville, and they are at Brownsville High School. I learn that Tom is having some difficulty with his mathematics. I use this in my next letter to Polly.

This paragraph is guaranteed so if it does not suit, I will take it back, postage prepaid. For the benefit of Brownsville High School and for a nice young man who could attain glory for his efforts in sports, I think you should help your friend pass his high school arithmetic. He may not be in danger of failing, but from all reports I have been receiving, if he doesn't snap out of it, he will not be eligible to play basketball next quarter. Of course, this is none of my business, but I hate to see people with such good possibilities fail because of such a little thing as passing a course.

There is no question that I may be treading on dangerous ground. This could well irritate Polly, but I have to try something. I still have strong feelings for her and seeing her only three or four times a year is killing me.

When I receive my next letter from home my reaction is, "This has really been a bad year." The first part of the news is good. The Baskins have purchased the empty brick bank building and are now back in the merchandise business. The second part of the news is bad. My family has purchased the house next door to the Paynes, one of two houses in Rocky Hill with indoor bathrooms. My immediate reaction is, "Polly will be at my house talking, laughing, singing with my sister more than she will be at home." It has been hard enough being considered by Polly simply as a good friend. Now it will be a next-door neighbor friend. If she gets any closer to my sister, she will probably adopt me as her brother. (Polly has no brothers or sisters.) Again, I am right. However, I simply can't think of Polly as my little sister.

When a fellow is busy in school and has daily responsibilities for housework and yard work, time passes very rapidly. In fact, I am moving rapidly through my business course. It is based on individual lessons. As soon as I finish a unit of study, I can take a test on this material, and if I make a grade of 90, I can proceed to the next unit. I finish the course in less than five months and begin looking for a job. Before my eighteenth birthday, I become a bookkeeper for the National Casket Company of Nashville, Tennessee.

I am not very proud of my degree, although I feel I have learned a lot of accounting. In fact, I feel cheated. However, I will never tell this to Polly. I have to admit that once I became my sole financial support, I approached life in a much different fashion. I have studied harder than I have ever studied before. It seems I am running out of time in my attempt to make Polly proud of me. No wonder I passed all the tests so quickly.

In searching for a job, I learn one important fact. To get one of the good jobs, or to get a job with unusual opportunity for advancement, you must have a college degree. If I am going to accomplish anything in life to make Polly proud of me, I must get a college degree. I have no idea how this will happen, but this becomes my goal.

Who can make plans? That which is happening right now, Sunday, December 7, 1941 will determine my life for the next five years. This day will probably be a stumbling block to all of my plans. In fact, this day is a soul-searching day in the lives of all young men in the United States. After Sunday school and church at the Belmont Heights Baptist Church, Randall, Sam, and I listen all afternoon to the radio account of the attack on Pearl Harbor by the Japanese. Sam Smith is a senior in high school who lives across the street.

> This is NBC with the latest news on the attack of Pearl Harbor by the Japanese. At 7:55 a.m. Hawaii time, unidentified planes were sighted over the skies of Oahu. By the time this information was communicated to the military it was too late. Waves of enemy torpedo-bomber planes attacked all of the military areas of Hawaii.
>
> There are seven battleships anchored in the harbor: the Arizona, California, Nevada, Oklahoma, Tennessee, Utah, and West Virginia. It has been reported that twenty-one ships have been sunk or damaged beyond repair, including all seven of the battleships. It has been estimated that over half of the four hundred aircraft located on Oahu have been destroyed.

We realize that this attack will change each of our lives in the days ahead. During the breaks for advertisements, we try to joke with comments such as:

"You will look good in khaki, Randall."

"Sam, I bet you are a hit with the girls in your navy white."

"I'll bet Buddy marches like he is plowing corn. His sergeant will really hate him."

Yes, we joke, but we know this is no joking matter. According to the radio reports, the United States is rapidly headed for war. This means that all young men have to place their lives on hold. The only thing that matters is winning the war.

It is Japan that has attacked the United States. Yet it seems from all radio accounts that we will be fighting the Germans. This is hard for us to understand. It seems that we may be fighting both Germany and Japan at the same time. Are we strong enough militarily to do this? To fight on two fronts will mean that all able-bodied men in the United States will be involved.

As we leave to purchase a hamburger for our evening meal, each of us comments on when we think we will be drafted. Since Randall works for a company that makes mine sweepers, he feels he will not be drafted for at least two years. Sam, being the youngest of the group, thinks it will be three years before he is drafted. I am the pessimist. I expect to be drafted within a year. When I comment I am trying to find a way to enroll in college before being drafted, my friends reply, "College? Why in the world would you want to go to college before being drafted? College won't help you pull the trigger on a gun."

"No, but I have read that there is a need for better educated people in the armed services. Some of us may need to go to college to help win the war. Anyway, where will I get enough money for college?"

This ends our conversation on the draft. My friends can't understand why anyone would be stupid enough to want to go to college when it is only a matter of time until we will all be drafted. Of course, they have no idea I am trying to impress Polly.

Time passes so rapidly. It will soon be time to go home for Christmas. I have received both a birthday card and a Christmas card from Polly. When I arrive home, Polly seems to be in a good humor with me. In fact, the old gang gets together one night at my house, and once again Polly is the life of the party. I have to behave myself because I have both an older sister and a "little sister" to keep me straight.

One night while at home, my old friend, M.G., comes by for a visit. We believe that one of Polly's friends, whom I once dated, is visiting her. I get the idea of going next door to arrange dates for the evening, M.G. with Polly and I with her friend. I reason that if I can't slow down the relationship between Polly and Tom, maybe someone else can be a stumbling block. The visit is made next door, but our information is incorrect. Polly's friend is not there. M.G. and I stay until bedtime anyway. It is a fun evening for me and affords something to discuss in my next letter to Polly.

Although I have not told Polly, I am determined to go to college. Actually, it is because of her that this is important. I want her to be proud of me. If I work at two jobs, I reason that I can save enough money before September for one year of college. Engineering schools usually have co-op programs for sophomores who have done well as freshmen. So I will major in engineering. Saving the money for college is quite a challenge. I take the first opportunity available for a second job, selling books and magazines for Collier Publishers. When I knock on the door and say I am working my way through college, I am telling the truth.

I give the person who answers the door my big country smile. "Good evening, I am Buddy Baskins, and I have some interesting opportunities to show you. May I come in?" Most of the time with my big smile and youthful look, I am invited to make my presentation.

First I survey the situation. If there are only older people, I talk about my medical book. If I am talking to a young couple without children, I usually emphasize magazines. If there are school age children around, my encyclopedia speech is apropos. I open a volume at a page on butterflies. With the children sitting on the floor with me looking at the beautiful pictures of butterflies, I ask, "Do you ever talk about butter-flies in school?" Usually there is a "Yes." I then point to a certain butterfly and ask, "Did you know that in the winter this butterfly flies all the way to Mexico to spend the winter where it is warm?" The eyes of the children get bigger. "Can you imagine this little butterfly flying all the way to Mexico?"

Then I turn to the section on Africa. "Have you studied about the wild animals of Africa?" When you study about them in school, all you have to do is turn to this page, and you have a picture of each animal." At this point I allow time for the children to really take a good look. Then I turn to the father and mother with my clincher. "Do you realize that you can have this encyclopedia consisting of sixteen books for only thirty-two cents a week?"

I hope I have aroused enough interest for the children to plead, "Oh Momma, can we have it?" Otherwise, I have to improvise, "In another five years, your children will have lost much of their enthusiasm for learning. Let's put the order into effect tonight." My supervisor calls me his "on the floor salesman." He says this with pride because I am making sales every evening and could become his outstanding part-time salesman.

Polly's letters mean a lot to me since I have no time for a social life.

> Did you hear Henry Aldrich last night? It has been the talk at school today. In case you did not hear, he was trying to find the definition of "syzygy." It was quite amusing. You mentioned the fact that you were listening to *Elmer's Tune*. I like that too, but *There'll Be Blue Birds Over the White Cliffs of Dover* and *Angels of Mercy* are my favorites.

> Our friend, M.G., came home with Paul Wednesday night to go sledding. He said he was almost scared to come back to Rocky Hill. I suppose I will never know just what took place Saturday night, December 27, 1941. It seems that everyone knows more about it than I. Perhaps it is better that way. I had no idea that everything was not perfectly on the level – that it was not just a friendly neighborly call until Monday morning on the bus when Paul laughingly said he could not wait to see old M.G. I soon smelled a mouse, and to my surprise M.G. really seemed to mind the teasing.

> One of the silliest things I've heard lately is that M.G. is struck on me. Can you imagine anything so absurd? Why he is no more struck on me, than – well pardon me

but – than you are. Why on earth is it that young people our age cannot get together and have fun (as I thought we were doing Saturday night) without the idea of courting being involved? .

Linden Avenue, Nashville, Tennessee, January 10, 1942. I do not know who gave you information about Saturday night, December 27, 1941 or what they told you. I agreed with M.G. that if Marge was at your house, we would ask the two of you for dates. When Marge was not there, I had fulfilled my part of the bargain. I enjoyed the evening very much.

As for M.G. being struck on you, my statement is this. Since you used a comparison, I will give it back to you. He likes you very much, but I cannot say whether it is the same way that I do or not. Only time will tell. Perhaps he could not take teasing or perhaps something else.

I am certain Polly will comment in her next letter on the last paragraph in my letter. However, I do not receive a letter from her for several weeks, and by that time she has either forgotten the statement or decides to ignore it. How unlucky can you get?

As soon as I master the routine of bookkeeping for the National Casket Company, I receive an additional assignment. My sales ability has been discovered, and they are ready to take advantage of it. The company is stingy with their money so the additional work assignment does not amount to much financially. However, I like the idea because it breaks the routine of sitting long hours at a time over a set of ledgers.

Next to the office suite, there is a large room with an elaborate display of caskets. Ordinarily, this display is visited by owners of funeral homes. However, occasionally someone wants a very expensive casket so the funeral director brings them to the display. The sales manager's desk is located by the front door, and he directs all visitations into the display area. My new assignment is to assist the sales manager. That is, when the sales manager is with a client, I serve the next visitor.

One day a funeral director arrives with an obviously wealthy lady, possibly in her late thirties. She is wearing a beautiful fur coat. The first thing that I notice is a ring with the biggest diamond I have ever seen.

"Can I help you?" I inquire.

"Yes," replies the funeral director. "Mrs. Watson wants to see your finest line of caskets for babies."

"Come this way please," as I direct them to the infant section of the display. "Mrs. Watson, this is the finest metal casket available. It is a copper lined inner seal steel casket and comes in four different colors. It costs only $400."

"I'll take it," Mrs. Watson responds. "I want the very best for Lulu."

I give instructors to the funeral director to take to billing and offer encouragement and comfort to Mrs. Watson. "How old was your baby?"

"She was eight years old."

I want to say, "This casket won't be large enough." Surely the funeral director would be aware of this.

"Was she sick for a long time?"

"No, only for a few days."

"I'm sure your daughter was very close to you."

"My daughter? She lives in Alaska. I have not seen her for three years."

"I mean the daughter who died."

"Young man, you are confused. It was Lulu, my beautiful Persian cat, that died."

The next morning, above my desk, is a big sign, "Star Salesman of Expensive Caskets for Cats." The office staff is really enjoying teasing me.

A note from my friend, Paul, in Rocky Hill causes me to evaluate again my feelings for Polly. Paul suspects that I like Polly more than just as a friend so he keeps me informed of the activities of Polly and Tom. In fact, the following news items appear in several different letters from friends.

> Polly and Tom are together so much at school that it seems natural in the junior play *Miss Adventure* they would play parts of the couple that would be married in the final scene.
>
> Another letter joked about the fact that Polly and Tom kissed five times during the play. Think of the fun they are having in practice.

It should have been obvious to me many months ago that my relationship with Polly is destined to be neighbor-friend (and possibly, big brother) and nothing more. In fact there is little chance that this will change, since I am at home only three or four times a year. What I need is a miracle. Polly has been a part of my prayers for many years. Now she becomes the focus of my prayers.

"Lord, I know if I ever have a chance with Polly, it will be because of Your graciousness. You know how I feel about her.

I would do anything You want me to do, if You would some-how help her to feel about me the way I feel about her. I would be a preacher, a missionary – just anything You want, Lord."

Very foolishly I try to bargain with the Lord.

I Belong To Uncle Sam

Near the end of April I visit Rocky Hill, leaving Nashville after work on Friday afternoon with plans to return Sunday afternoon. I hate to miss the possible sales of books and magazines on Friday night and Saturday, but I need a break from work. Polly is in and out of the house visiting with my sister several times on Saturday. I am expecting her to be there, so I go prepared. I have my saxophone and sheet music for new popular songs. I have already transcribed the music so I can play the songs on the saxophone. "Polly, I have an experiment to suggest if you have time?"

"What's the experiment?"

"I brought my saxophone. Want to see if we can play together?"

"Sure. What are the songs?'

"Here are two sheets of music."

"Say, these are my favorites. They look awfully hard. I probably can't play them."

"That's okay. I probably can't play with a piano, but it might be fun trying."

"Let's give it a try."

Well, we do have fun with our experiment, but no listener would have called it music. The important thing is that I am alone with Polly for over two hours. This visit generates several letters from Polly, and these are appreciated at this time. With my two jobs, there is no time for a social life.

Dear Buddy,

I enjoyed very much playing music with you last Saturday. I do wish I could take some more music lessons. Really, I don't know how your family puts up with me, but I can't keep from getting lonely especially since school is out.

I'm so glad you are doing well. Perhaps it will show some of the oldsters here that the younger generation is not so bad.

Polly and I correspond several times during the summer, but always as good friends. Her letters are so cordial during this period I might have been able to change our relationship if I could have gone home four or five times during the summer; however, I must have the book sales on Friday nights and Saturdays if there is to be money for college in the fall. After all, this extra effort is planned to make Polly proud of me. I am tempted several times to tell her of my love for her. However, I am sure my love would be rejected, and this would hurt the close friendship between our two families.

A letter from Polly on August 17, 1942 indicates she has started her senior year in high school.

> I guess I have forfeited all claim on your friendship, and my name is now probably among your list of unknowns, but nevertheless I'm making a feeble attempt to deserve at least another letter. There is little evidence of life in Rocky Hill from 7:30 a.m. to 5:00 p.m. since August 10 when school started. There are twenty-two seniors but only four boys.
>
> Please don't think I've been doing unto others, as I'd have them do unto me by not writing you. I believe you have really forgotten Rocky Hill this time.

There may be eighteen senior girls for only four senior boys, but you, Polly, have nothing to worry about. You have your steady, Tom, and he is crazy about you. You will have a wonderful year.

I have a successful summer selling books and magazines in the evening, and the income from these sales along with my regular salary at the National Casket Company enable me to save the necessary money to begin my engineering training at the Speed Scientific School of the University of Louisville. My high school buddy, Paul Cramer, has shown the University catalog to Sis and Polly, and they both comment that the curriculum seems a bit difficult for graduates of Brownsville High School. Of course, this opinion serves as a challenge to Paul and me. So we rent a room on Third Street and enroll as freshmen at the University of Louisville in mid-September, 1942. We cook on a hot plate in our room, and occasionally grab a hamburger nearby.

✧

After fifteen months in Nashville, several facts are evident about my life. The social life of most young people in the city involves activities that are foreign to me. In Rocky Hill, there were no opportunities to learn to dance, swim, bowl, skate, or play cards. These are common activities on dates in the city. This inadequacy, plus working day and night, plus my failure to develop any type of relationship with Polly except as a next-door neighbor friend begin to affect my personality. I seem to be developing an inferiority complex and becoming more shy in the presence of young ladies. I know I have to overcome this difficulty, but there seems to be no time to work on the problem. This has to change.

I work until just a few days before time to enroll at the University of Louisville, so I spent very little time in Rocky Hill. I do see Polly a couple of times when she comes across the yard to see Sis. For some reason she does not seem as friendly as usual. I wonder if it has anything to do with Tom. To me one thing is certain. God evidently is not interested in bargaining with me.

As I leave for Louisville, I decide I must face the truth about my relationship with Polly. My feelings for her are having way too much effect on my life. So I take the problem to the Lord in prayer. My daily prayers include asking the Lord to decrease the influence on my life caused by my feelings for Polly.

I believe in prayer and fully expect the Lord to answer my prayers by helping me overcome my feelings for her. However, there seems to be one more step necessary to go with my prayers. I believe the Bible teaches you need to confess wrong actions before praying about them. I try to accomplish this in a letter to Polly.

2013 3rd Street, Louisville, September 23, 1942.
Before heading for Louisville I was looking through some of my old papers and guess what I saw. Three letters were tied up in a nice bundle. These were saved from the note-writing calamity during my first semester at Brownsville.

As I remember that semester, it went something like this: A boy, who was really shy around girls, goes to school in another town, falls for a certain girl, and does not know how to express it. (I guess it would be called puppy love.) So he writes notes to her. In comes the villain (a perfect novel), who gets the notes and distributes them throughout school, even giving one to the girl's father. The poor boy's heart is broken.

He does not know whether to run away from home or join the army. Well, he cannot decide so he writes a nasty letter to the girl. He is still in love with this girl; yet, his only reaction is to tease her. I want to apologize for teasing you and the difficulty I have caused you. Now you know the reason for the hard teasing. I was so in love with you I could not stand to see you with someone else.

To a certain extent, I am glad it all happened. If it had not happened, I might still be trying to fulfill my desire for "puppy love" like some people I know today. It all hurt so very much at the time because I really fell hard for you. I trust that this will be good for me in the long run because I can now lay aside childish nonsense and start my happy-go-lucky, never-a-worry life.

I am still dumb about things of the heart. I really had expected Polly to give some reaction to my admission that I fell in love with her a few years earlier. Would her reaction have been any different if I had told her I still loved her. Probably not! She does not mention in her reply that I said I was once deeply in love with her. She may have known all along that I loved her or she does not care either way. It is probably the latter. The main topic of her reply is a description of how mean I have been by teasing her. She twists my words to imply that I have no interest in her now in any way other than as a friend. Just my luck, I strike out again.

Although I am no theologian, I believe a prayer has a much better chance of being answered if one shows faith by making a distinct effort to accomplish what is requested in the prayer. I determine I will find time for dates with lovely young ladies in the days ahead. This is the way to forget Polly. Secondly, just as soon as I can find time, I am going to study and research the psychology of women. I have learned, with little talent, how to become a good baseball player. I have learned how to be a good salesman. There is no reason in the world why I can't learn how to be well liked by the opposite sex. I have a lot to learn, but I intend to succeed.

My intentions are good, but I still have a lot to learn about women. In fact, Paul and I try to go big time too soon. What a flop! Much to the surprise of our families we have very good grades at mid-term. Thus we are invited to pledge Triangle Fraternity. This fraternity is really a social fraternity, but they select as pledges students with better than average grades in the first quarter of their freshman year.

The big event is a dance in honor of the pledges. Paul and I debate at length how to handle this affair. We finally decide to allow the fraternity to arrange for dates with a couple of pledges of a sorority. The biggest problem is that we have never been to a dance. Dancing was considered a sin in Rocky Hill and Brownsville, so very few of the young people know how to dance. Yet, we feel the need to participate in this activity since it seems to be connected with our grades. Paul's aunt agrees to show us some dance steps, and after a couple of short lessons, we are ready to go.

Now our dates would never have won beauty contests at the University of Louisville. Paul comments, "I saw at least three other dates more homely than ours." However, they were great sports because we step on their toes all evening. They are such good sports that we feel they deserve a good meal after the dance. Both dates live in a suburban area located as far as you can go and still be in the city. The taxi fare is unreal. When we get back to our room, I comment to Paul that I have learned one thing. I do not have enough money to live the fraternity life. The dance, the meal, the taxi fare have used my allowance for the whole month.

At Christmas, one quarter of the engineering school year is complete, and I think I have made fairly good grades. I guess that this might be my last quarter in college. Two things are evident. If I do not change my spending habits, I will not have enough money for four quarters. Actually, this does not matter, because the draft board is needing me to fill their quota. Most of my high school friends my age are being deferred until they finish high school.

While at home for Christmas, I tell Mom and Dad what I have in mind. The army air force has a plan whereby I can get twelve months of college. Since I have been paying my own way, this looks great to me. It is interesting to note how much I have matured from the time I left home eighteen months ago until now. I could not wait to get away from home in June, 1941, but now I want to make things easier for Mom and Dad. They suggest that I discuss my plans with their neighbor, Mr. Payne (Polly's father). Frankly, I am just being considerate because I have already completed the application for the air force.

One night all of the old gang gets together for fun, food, and tales. Polly is there and seems to enjoy herself even though her boyfriend was not invited.

Soon after returning to Louisville, I receive the following memorandum from Headquarters, Army Air Forces, Washington D.C, January 16, 1943.

> "You have been found to have the educational qualifications for pre-meteorological training with the Army Air Forces. In order to take advantage of this opportunity for training, it will be necessary for you to arrange with your local selective service board for your voluntary induction into the army. If you volunteer for induction, you should endeavor to have your induction accomplished within 15 days."

You should have seen the expression on the faces of the Brownsville Selective Service Board when I ask to be drafted in fifteen days. "You mean you are ready to go in fifteen days? Everyone else wants their induction delayed." I finally have to explain the reason for my request. I have to have an immediate induction to get in the program for which I have volunteered.

I have no idea why I was selected for the meteorology program. The brochure plainly states that only those students who have two years of college with good grades, or graduates from outstanding prep programs are eligible. I do not meet either of these criteria. In addition, it states that applicants should have completed solid geometry, advanced algebra, and trigonometry along with physics in either high school or college. I have had none of these courses. I really am not eligible for this program. The selection must have been made before my high school transcript arrived. Perhaps I received some good recommendations from my professors at the University of Louisville, or maybe my prayers are being answered these days. Yes, I realize that this program might be a little difficult for me since I do not have the appropriate prerequisites. However, I have nothing to lose, as I will be drafted soon. So I'll give it a try.

In the middle of January, I check out of the University of Louisville, receive my tuition refund, which I immediately place in my bank account before spending it, and become a soldier in the army air force. On February 1, 1943 I report to local board number 37 at Brownsville, Kentucky.

There is an opportunity, in passing, to say good-bye to Polly and to congratulate her on her birthday. Time passes so rapidly. My cute little freckle-faced Polly is now sweet sixteen. She is a hit with all my friends who have not yet graduated from high school. She is good-looking; downright cute actually, possesses a pleasant personality, and is well liked by all, male and female. She is still a devoted Christian. There is just one problem. She and Tom are just as "steady" as ever.

It is not as easy as I thought to leave for the army. It is not like leaving for Nashville or Louisville. In fact, at some point down the road, it is possible that I will be placing my life on the line for my country. Right now, I am proud of this opportunity.

A New Way Of Life

As I leave for the army, I go fully determined to get Polly out of my mind. I am convinced now that there is no way we can be anything other than good friends. As I face the new life in the army, I will also face a new life without Polly.

My new life is certainly different. No one can accuse the army of trying to make a soldier look well dressed. My first issue of army clothes is so large I can barely keep my pants up, and the shoes cannot be laced tight enough to keep them from slipping up and down on my narrow heels. It is my shoes that finally persuade me to walk back to the supply room and ask for smaller sizes. I know I am going to experience difficulty with the supply sergeant, but I have no desire for blisters. First I show him that my shoes are too large. He has some sympathy for foot problems, so he gives me a smaller pair of shoes. They are still too wide, but the length is just about right. With this bit of success I have the courage to ask for smaller clothes. The sergeant growls at me, but for some reason he seems to like my big smile so I now have somewhat smaller uniforms.

It is hard for me to realize I have been away from home for nineteen months as I enter the army air force at Keesler Air Force Base, Mississippi. However, I am not prepared for the verbal filth and sinful lifestyle at basic training. The drill sergeant can't say two words without taking the Lord's name in vain. The language in the barracks is worse. Most conversations are about sex exploits. I keep wondering if this is typical of all units of the military. How can God bless an army composed of so much filth?

I enjoy marching - that is, after I learn my right foot from my left foot. It is fun to march and sing: "Off we go into the wild blue yonder, climbing high into the sky, . . ." or "I've got a six pence, a jolly, jolly six pence. I've got a six pence to last me all my life . . ." or "Bell-bottomed trousers, coats of navy blue, he'll climb the rigging like his daddy used to do . . .." It is even more fun to run in formation and sing at the same time. I am in good condition in comparison to some of the fellows from the city.

I do not tell anyone, because in the army the barracks must be filled with gripes and complaints, but I enjoy the challenge of the obstacle course. I like trying to determine the easiest way to overcome a given obstacle. I also enjoy the shooting range. I grew up with a rifle and a shotgun. I hate the barracks. Soldiers try to drown their unhappiness at being in the army by drinking cheap beer. Loudness is always the name of the game. Usually some drunken soldier is trying to pick a fight. I stay out of trouble by saying, "Can't you see by my smile that I am your friend?" A few beers seem to loosen a soldier's tongue to release a lifetime of curse words. It sounds as if everyone in my barracks is training to be a drill sergeant.

I finally locate the camp library or reading room. This enables me to get away from the barracks. It also gives me an opportunity to think about improving my understanding of girls. I am serious about this goal in my life. I realize I am a failure with girls because there are so many things that I do not do well, such as dancing. To counteract this lack of social skills, I need to develop such a great personality that my weaknesses will not be noticed. A summary of my plans for improvement are glued to the inside lid of my footlocker:

> Girls will be an integral part of my life in the days ahead. I will work to make my association with them pleasing to them. Most girls like to feel appreciated, and like recognition. I will work to find something unique and fascinating about each date. Then I will introduce this as a topic of conversation. I will treat each date (pretty or ugly) as if she were the queen for a day.

I sincerely believe that if I can do these things my relationship with girls will reach a new plateau. I even ask the Lord to help me become a new Buddy Baskins. Also there is another reason for this effort. One day I want Polly to discover the new Buddy, so she will know what she has missed.

In early March, 1943, I leave Biloxi for the State University of Iowa at Iowa City for twelve months of concentrated work in mathematics and science in preparation for meteorology. Imagine my surprise when I see my new home away from home. My company, consisting of eight platoons, resides in the beautiful Law of Commons dormitory. In ordinary times, this building houses the School of Law.

I am warned that most of the cadets in this program have had two or three years of work in big universities or are from outstanding preparatory programs. Although my grades are good enough to get me into this program, Brownsville High School is not academically one of the great schools in Kentucky. Whoever heard of physics or chemistry at Brownsville High School? We are constantly reminded each quarter that the fifteen percent with the lowest test scores in the class might be dropped from the program to become foot soldiers. I do not plan for that to happen to me. This is too good an opportunity for first-class university work at no cost to me.

I am now certain that being stationed at the State University of Iowa is an answer to my prayers. I have prayed for a better relationship with girls in general as a means of forgetting my feelings for Polly. The Lord has answered my prayers by placing me in a "Garden of Eden." Every Saturday night there is some activity involving girls at the Student Union Building of the University. This provides ample opportunities to practice improving my relationship with girls. In any experimental process there are usually a lot of failures before success. An occasional success does provide encouragement.

The first big test of my improvement involves a dance hosted by the School of Nursing. For this dance it is a cute redhead who catches the attention of the cadets. I am interested in checking my learning progress, but I decide to wait until the competition decreases a bit. A close friend in my platoon, Stan Sullinger, has red hair and is just about the same height as the girl. He has been "swapping out" with others all night, and seems to be winning the competition. It is obvious he is planning to hold her hand on the way to the hospital residence hall.

As I cut in I explain, "My dancing is pretty awkward. I grew up in the country."

"You did? Me too." Beth replies with a smile.

"Really?"

"I grew up on a farm forty miles from Ames, Iowa."

"What kind of farm?"

"A dairy farm. We had twenty milking machines. Dad would place the feed for each cow. My brother and I would attach the milking machines."

By this time Stan is back for his turn. While they dance I plan my strategy. I decide I will emphasize the country theme. Stan is surprised when I cut in. He looks at me with a confident smile, which suggests, "You don't have a chance, Baskins."

I learn Beth is dreadfully homesick. We discuss the fun she has had at home in the country, and before she realizes what is happening, we are having a great time just talking about her experiences.

It is great holding hands with the cute little redhead as we meander across campus to the hospital area where the School of Nursing is located. I learn far more about Iowa farms than I want to know, but the kiss at the end of the trail is well worth my trouble.

Stan cannot understand what happened to him last night. Beth seemed to like him. "Why did she go for you, Buddy? You are a clumsy dancer." "Maybe someday I will tell you, Stan."

I am working hard to become a charming soldier. At the same time I have no interest in any girl except as a friend. This activity does seem to keep my mind off Polly. I still have to work hard to keep Polly out of my mind.

Well, either the Lord is answering my prayers in a way I do not expect or Polly is angry with me, or she is getting seriously involved in her courtship with Tom. I have received few letters from her the last three months. I surmise that Polly is reading all of my letters to my sis, so I manage to mention a lovely young lady in each letter. I do not want her to think I am sitting in my barracks "pining away." Then I receive news from Rocky Hill that requires a letter to Polly.

State University of Iowa, May 20, 1943. How do you like being a high school graduate? It is not so hot, is it? Congratulations! I read with pride the article in the county paper saying, "Miss Polly Payne of Rocky Hill, Kentucky received the highest scholarship award at the Brownsville High School graduation." Of course, this is what I expected.

Did you ever have something to say, but could not find the appropriate words with which to say it? This is the way I am now. Today I got a letter from my sis. In that letter she mentioned that she had read a copy of your letter to me describing how mean I once was to you. I would rather have had anybody under the sun read that than to have had her read it. But it is too late now. A few months ago I would have gotten angry and would have written a nasty letter or something of the sort, but last fall I told you I would never do that again.

My sis was thoroughly disgusted with me. In fact, it seems that you certainly did burst her hopes that I might be a real gentleman. There could be a few points on my side, but for once I will try to be unselfish and keep my mouth shut because I would not want to say or do anything that would hurt your and her friendship.

So, please forget all about this letter and don't mention it to Sis. The thing I want you to remember is: I want to beg of you as friend to friend and neighbor to neighbor, please don't show any more of the old letters we have written than you feel is necessary. If I was as mean as you said, I do not want anyone to know about it. I believe you will do your best to grant this favor, and I wish to say, "Thanks a million." Always your friend, Buddy

My letter to Polly gets an immediate reply. In fact, she apologizes for sharing our letter writing with my sister. She explains that, while she was house cleaning, she found the scribbled copy of the masterpiece, and it sounded so childish and comical that she couldn't resist sharing it with someone. Since she depends so much on my sis for many things, she shared it with her. Then she said, "I'm sorry, terribly sorry." Finally, she gets to what I want to hear. She promises never to show any more of our old letters to anyone. For some reason I seem to be happy that Polly and I are corresponding again.

The first quarter finally ends in late June, 1943, and I head home for a few days. I do not let anyone know I am getting a furlough because I am not certain that I will get one. Examinations for all students in the pre-meteorology program are compiled and graded at the University of Chicago. I believe I know a bit more than the lower fifteen percent of the cadets at SUI. However, SUI might not be typical of all programs. With these uncertainties, it seems better not to mention a furlough to anyone because those who are being dropped from the program will go immediately to the infantry without a furlough.

It is a big relief to receive the furlough orders. I rationalize, "Well, I am good for three more months at SUI." On the train headed for Kentucky, I have plenty of time to think. My sister will be in the mountains of Kentucky doing missionary work, so Polly will not be in and out of the house as usual. Although my feelings for Polly no longer cause me difficulty, she is still close to my heart. I know much about her activities through my correspondence with others. This is her third year to go steady with Tom. One letter to me comments, "They do everything together." Another letter states that nearly all of Polly's graduation pictures are pictures with Tom. Will I get to talk to Polly at all? I would like to be with her for a few minutes at some time while I am at home. However, I have to be very careful. Tom is exceedingly jealous of me. I certainly do not want to cause her any difficulty.

It is a dark, rainy night when I walk the mile from Highway 31, where I get off a bus, into Rocky Hill. It is so dark that, without a light, I have to feel my way along the edge of the highway. As a guide I place one foot off the pavement and one foot on the pavement. My right foot encounters several mud holes. My parents have been asleep for some time when I knock on the door. Mother is so excited. This is the first time she has seen her son in uniform (in fact, a wet uniform). I expect Mom and Dad to go back to bed, but both are now trying to talk at the same time. They have so much to say to me. I finally make them go to bed, because they have to work in the store tomorrow.

With my parents working and Sis not at home, I am expecting a long, dreary week. Just the opposite happens. When Polly learns I am at home, she takes over, and my furlough becomes a wonderful, restful period. This is what I very much need.

I wonder how Polly will explain this week to Tom. It soon becomes evident. She has adopted me as her big brother; that is, she is assuming the role of "little sis." If I were Tom, I would ask, "How stupid can you get?"

Since Mom and Dad are at the store much of the time, it is not appropriate for Polly to visit me at our house. So we spend most of the week on an old quilt pallet under a big maple tree that divides the two yards. At night we sit in a swing on Polly's porch, and if some of my friends come by for a visit, Polly serves popcorn and lemonade. Thursday morning she bakes a chocolate pie. Boy, oh boy, it is good!

Of course, the most enjoyable times occur when we are alone. We talk long and late about hopes and dreams for the future. Polly wants very much to attend a certain Baptist college. Her parents will have to borrow the money for her to attend college, and the tuition is simply too much at the college she prefers. I truly want the best for Polly. "I hope you get to go to the college of your choice, but if you don't, I hope you get to attend some Baptist college. You have so much to offer the world."

Then I share with her my uncertainties about army life. I have not discussed my army situation with anyone at home, but for some reason I tell her of being in a program for which I am not really qualified. She replies, "It is a shame for a high school to shortchange a person with your ability and ambition." I explain that it is possible that I might be dropped from the program. "When I return to SUI, I will have my scores in comparison to all scores on all campuses. Then I will know my standing."

"Buddy, you have nothing to worry about. You can do anything you want to do."

"I wish it were that simple," is my reply.

One day we enjoy a light-hearted discussion of the person each of us will marry. I declare that Polly will marry a Reverend Peterson. I explain that she is a natural for a preacher's wife, with her unusual musical ability.

"Is he ugly?" she asks.

"Oh no! He is very handsome. He is a bit skinny at six feet four inches. As he grows older, he will probably take on weight and be just right."

"Tell me more," she requests with a twinkle in her eye.

"He has a wonderful personality; he is always smiling; he is well liked by all."

"Sounds good."

"He has a very strong voice. There will be no sleeping when he is preaching."

"Will we be in a city church or a country church?"

"Neither. You two will form an evangelistic team, traveling all over the United States, winning the lost to the Lord. Just think of all the places you will see in your travels." On and on Polly asks her questions as I spin a tale about her future husband.

Polly jokes, "I'll need your help in finding such a special person." I wonder if she notices that none of my descriptions of her husband fit in any way the personality of Tom.

"Let me tell you about Maggie, your future wife. She is small, very cute, and is extremely energetic. She is a bit selfish and does not want you to glance at another girl. You will have to be very careful," is the beginning of Polly's description of my future wife.

"Does she love me?"

"Oh, very much. You two are very, very happy. You are known as the love bugs in your town."

"How do I make a living?"

Polly's answer is quick and to the point. "After the war you return to college and graduate with a major in mathematics. You are known as an outstanding teacher at Brownsville High School."

An immediate thought is, "Is this what she would like for me to do?" I continue asking questions, and Polly's imagination about life with Maggie seems to be unlimited. Several times during the week we play tennis in the street, the only place available in our little town. We both have a great time.

The week flies by, and for the last night of the furlough the Baptist preacher and his wife invite a young married couple and us to their house for dinner. I ask Polly, "Will this be okay with Tom?" "Why do you ask such a stupid question?" is her answer.

Brother Pierce keeps us laughing throughout the evening. He is a natural comedian, and we have a great time. I am the perfect gentleman. I cannot make a mistake in front of my "little sis." We walk to the Pierces in early evening, but we return in a car with the young married couple. The night is beautiful; there is a full moon. What a wonderful opportunity for romance, if I were not with my "little sis." How I long to hold her hand, but somehow I control myself.

At the door I explain, "As you know, I will be leaving tomorrow on train number eight. It is good to get home and see Mom and Dad, but as much as they have to work in the store, I felt it was going to be a lonely week. Then along comes a wonderful person and makes my lonely week into a perfect one. Thank you so very much. Good-bye and good luck in college. I'll be praying for you to go to a Baptist college." It seems that Polly is about to cry. Is she taking this little sis business a bit too far?

As I walk across the yard to my house, I realize, "I've never been with a girl as much as I have been with Polly this week. Thank you, Lord, for helping me control my feelings for her. I would not want to do anything that would hurt our good friendship. I hope Tom does not give her a hard time. However, the truth is I am still madly in love with her. I probably will always love her. I guess I will just have to learn to live with it and be satisfied being a good friend."

Polly Goes To College

All good things come from God. This I was taught at home by word and action. So when I return to Iowa City, I express thanks to God for the good things that are happening to me. I am overjoyed with the Chicago report. My grades are above the fiftieth percentile of all students in the program. I just cannot believe the good news. If I continue to study, I have no need to fear being dropped from the program.

I finally find time after starting a new quarter at SUI to write Polly.

From Iowa City, summer, 1943. Did I have fun last night! I thought I was improving a little , but after last night I guess I am just as mean as ever. It was very hot in Iowa City, especially on the third floor, so three soldiers crawl through their windows to the fire escape where they make their bunks and plan to sleep.

All is going well until a certain soldier looks out his window (guess who?). He quickly sees the harm that could come to them if they should happen to roll in their sleep. Being a humanitarian, he begins making plans for their safety. A quick search is made for water containers, and all windows by the fire escape are fastened. Even before this is accomplished, several others volunteer to help on this life-saving project.

At exactly 11:30 p.m. it starts raining, and what a downpour! There is one simulated roll of thunder as a dropped metal trashcan hits the steel railing of the fire escape. All at once the snoring stops. Through the rain one can see three scantily clad soldiers rushing up the steps of the fire escape for their rooms, and @#$^*& each of them shouts as he tries to open his window, but it is securely fastened. What a rain! It does not stop until the three soldiers rush all the way down the escape, and jump three feet into a mud hole below the escape.

This humanitarian, having done his duty, quickly but silently hides all water containers, closes the door to his room, places three sturdy chairs against it, jumps into bed, and immediately begins snoring. Then comes a knock, a push, and a shove. Finally, this activity stops with the angry remark, "He would have to barricade his door."

In closing, Polly, there is no way I can describe my visit home. With Sis in the mountains and Mom and Dad busy at the store, I expected an uneventful week. Instead you made it into a superb week. It was great just sitting and talking to you on the porch and under the maple tree. I don't know whether my friends came by to see me or to enjoy the refreshments. You were more than neighborly; you were kind, sweet, and wonderful. Words are inadequate to express my appreciation.

✧

For months I have been asking God to relieve me of some of my feelings for Polly. It is terrible being in love with someone who considers you only as a good friend. God seems to be answering my prayers. Our appreciation for each other as friends and next-door neighbors is growing with time. I do not particularly care for the "little sister" relationship, but evidently I have no choice.

I also ask God to help me develop a better relationship with girls in general. I have no desire for a serious relationship. I simply desire friendship. I am certain this will help me keep my mind off Polly. Again God seems to be answering my prayers. Many weekends I stay on campus. Other times I take a trolley with five or six buddies to the neighboring city of Cedar Rapids. We go as a group because sleeping three to a bed (crossways) and six to a room, our hotel accommodations are inexpensive. Since there are no military camps located near Cedar Rapids, on Saturday afternoon the downtown is filled with lovely girls, all appreciative of soldiers. This provides unusual opportunities for me to improve my relationship with girls.

However, I am a loner in some of my trips to Cedar Rapids. Sometimes I do my studying on Saturday and Saturday night, saving my trip to Cedar Rapids for Sunday morning. I visit several churches and select one that has a strong youth program. My goal is to attend the youth fellowship in the evening. Most of the time I am the only soldier in attendance. Although I am nineteen, I can easily pass for fifteen or sixteen. Always there are activities after the youth program. I try to get an invitation from a group going to some home. Why? I hope that they will dance.

I explain I am from a rural area and not much of a dancer. I would really appreciate their help. It is fantastic. After I have danced with a girl, all (both boys and girls) tell me what I need to do to improve. The first time this happens I expect to be embarrassed. Instead, the youngsters make it a fun situation. "You need to be a bit more aggressive in leading your partner." Leon suggests. "Don't be bashful. Sometimes Amy is leading you." "Also hold her closer to you," adds Tom. "I'd like that," I reply with a big laugh. "But not too close," cautions Amy. After my dance with Lori, Leon, the most vocal of the group suggests, "Loosen up. Dancing is fun. You are making it look like work. Get the rhythm and swing with it." I am beginning to learn how to dance. Ray and his date drive me to the station to catch the trolley. They are kind and considerate in their comments, "Buddy, you sure learned a lot about dancing tonight. Come back two or three more times, and we will make a real dancer out of you." I answer, "You are a great group. Thanks for bringing me to the station."

In addition to finally learning to dance a bit, I have the opportunity to date some of the finest Christian girls in Cedar Rapids. This I had not expected. I never ask for a date until I think the family knows me. Also, I try not to ask any girl for a date who seems to have a regular boyfriend. I do not want the guys unhappy with me. I have to learn how to dance. First, I ask Lori, "How about having dinner with me next Saturday night and a movie afterwards? I'll stay overnight in a hotel, and I'll meet you at church Sunday morning."

"I'd love to, but I will have to ask my parents. It will probably be okay since they seem to like you."

It is great "showing off" my high school dates to the other cadets. I really enjoy being seen with charming girls like Lori. I arrange to meet my cadet friends and their dates for dinner. Then Lori and I leave the group and head for a movie. Since I am with their daughter at church, Lori's father and mother feel obligated to invite a soldier to go home with them for lunch. Those Iowa women sure know how to cook, and this old Kentucky boy really appreciates a home-cooked meal.

Polly finally answers my letter inquiring about her college status. She has been in Cincinnati visiting a cousin. In this letter she gives me the good news. In about twenty days she will be entering Campbellsville College. She explains it is a Baptist junior college. I am pleased to learn that Polly has been admitted to a Baptist college since this has been her wish all through high school. I want the best for her. Polly concludes her letter with:

> I bet it will be ages before I get to see you again because if you should happen to get a furlough, I'll be away in school. But maybe we might have a vacation at the same time. Here's hoping.
> Your substitute sis, Polly

I enjoy Polly's entire letter except the closing. I've got to work on that. I do not feel like her big brother.

A card from a friend brings me up-to-date on the latest gossip. There are no secrets in a small town like Rocky Hill. This summer has been a difficult summer for Polly and Tom. Soon Polly will be leaving for college, and a bit later Tom will be drafted in the army. They are together at least once a week.

Tom drives the mail truck for his dad during the summer and goes through Rocky Hill twice a day, slowing down a bit for a wave of the hand and a longing look if Polly is outside, and she often is, because she well knows the mail truck's schedule.

At the end of the second quarter, I do not expect much of a furlough. Sis will leave for the mission field in the mountains of Kentucky soon after my arrival. Polly is supposed to leave for college before I get there. I feel it is going to be a long week.

I arrive home late Sunday afternoon. For some reason Polly has not yet left for Campbellsville College. In fact, she is on her last date with Tom before leaving. I see Polly early Monday morning as she is loading the car to leave. It is great to see her and to wish her success and happiness in college, but I keep thinking, "If she had been at home last night, we could have had a great time talking – you know, friend to friend and neighbor to neighbor."

When Sis leaves for the mission field, I decide to spend the last days of my furlough doing good things for people. First, I think of Polly. She has been very close to her mother and dad. She even got homesick after a week with her cousin in Cincinnati. I surmise she is going to be one "homesick little girl" in about two weeks. What can I do to offer her cheer in her first days away from home? All of a sudden I have an idea. When I left home, she compiled for me a newspaper called the Rocky Hill News. I look for the old typewriter I once gave the family. There are only two keys that seem to stick. So I start for her a four-page newspaper, three columns to a page.

Home-Town Girl Makes Good
People stood in their doors with open mouths; all eligible bachelors peeped around corners of houses with sad

faces, while the fair damsels wished to be in her shoes. Tears could be seen streaming down some of the cheeks of on-lookers, but everyone was happy in Rocky Hill Monday morning.

Why? Because Rocky Hill's number one citizen was leaving for college. Of course, we hated to lose her, but we knew it was for the best. The G.A. girls will miss her, the Rocky Hill Baptist Church will miss her, the church youth group will miss her, Rocky Hill Elementary School will miss her, Brownsville High School will miss her. In fact, everything will miss her, even the grass under the big maple tree, the grass she so often used as a featherbed. To her we extend our best wishes, and she can always be sure that she will be remembered in our prayers.

I feel her college friends will expect something romantic. Since it is not appropriate for me to write such to someone who considers me just a good friend, I need to use a fictitious love story.

Rocky Hill's One and Only Love Story

To Mary with Love,

"I love you so much, darling." I stopped pecking at the typewriter and looked around nervously. It was a pretty good letter so far, I thought. Not too much goo, but pretty solid, enough to let her know she was important and loved.

This was the fourth letter to Mary this week. It was dog-gone tough finding new words of endearment and new words of love to write her. There was nothing wrong with the old standbys, of course. "I love you madly," I add. "And I think of you from reveille to taps, just like the song says."

I looked up and grinned. This was good stuff, especially from a soldier. Women went for it. Mary did anyway. I scratched my head, lifted the portable typewriter from my lap and went to the footlocker. I opened it and looked steadily at Mary's picture pinned on the lid. It was 8x10 colored. "Wow, she is beautiful." I whispered, and looked around guiltily. Nobody was watching.

I closed the locker and went back to my bunk. Then perched the typewriter on my lap and continued. "Every time I look at your picture, the thought of your beauty runs through my blood like sweet wine. Your name is like a golden bell hung in my heart, and when I think of you it rings and sings, Mary, Mary."

"I love you. I adore you. What more can I say?" As a matter of fact, there was little more I could say. I was running dry. "It is you I am fighting for. You are my war aims, my hopes."

I closed the typewriter with a bang. "The heck with this," I said to myself. "These letters are getting too tough. It will cost the Sarge ten bucks a letter next month, or he'll have to write his own love letters, and say pretty things to sweeten up Mary."

One day while on leave, I drive to Brownsville to see my old baseball team play a local rival. I see Tom at the game. I know he will write Polly that he saw me; I need to mention him in this newspaper. So I write a short article on sports. Our mutual friend, M.G. Sumpter, married during the summer immediately after graduating from high school. Such marriages were typical at this time.

Sports

Brownsville High School must have used a secret weapon last Tuesday as they won a 17-4 victory over the Kyrock baseball nine. M.G. Sumpter umpired the game. Could this have affected the score?

Looking in the stands, I quickly spied Mrs. Sumpter. She seemed to be quite thrilled with the way her husband was umpiring the game, but you should have seen the angry look on her face when a Kyrock player disagreed with one of the ump's decisions.

Everyone at the game seemed to be happy. No, wait a minute! Look at that good looking chap with black curly hair, sitting on the end of the stands. "Say bud. Why are you so sad?" You are not sad. Okay. Wait a minute. Look at that forced smile. He is sad because his girl friend is away in college, but his pride will not let him show it.

I know I will not get many letters from Polly at college. First she has to write Tom. Then she needs to write home. She must find time for writing to two girl friends (including my sister). Maybe I will be fifth or sixth on her list, but some day I expect a letter. It happens in six weeks.

You clever rascal! Never again will I ever attempt anything unique in regard to you because you always come back with something so much more clever. That newspaper was honestly the most enjoyable epistle I ever received. It certainly came at an opportune time and served a worthwhile cause. I was one of the most homesick "little" girls those first days that ever was, and your letter came at the right time to provide cheer. I laughed and laughed until the whole dorm wanted to know what had come over me.

Then she describes her final weekend with Tom. I guess her big brother needs to hear all about this:

I stayed three weeks before going home, and it seemed like three months. Tom had some extra gas so he brought me back. We brought Mom and Dad and Opal back with us, and we really had fun. I hated to see them leave. That was the last time I saw Tom before he left for the army.

I do much better than Polly. I answer her letter in three weeks. I guess she is a bit lonesome, because we exchange letters about every three weeks after this.

Just before the end of the third quarter my company receives the bad news. The air force has already trained enough meteorologists to meet needs for the next ten years. Cadets in this program will have opportunities to select areas that might utilize their special training. Many of the cadets are selecting areas such as radar, electronics, and research. I do not want a desk job in the army. How can I make Polly proud of me with a desk job? I have until after my next furlough to make my selection, but I already know what I will choose. I want to fly a P-38 fighter plane, so I select flying duty.

At the time of my leave on December 23, I am beginning to achieve with the better students. I have no worry about not getting a furlough. This is a special Christmas at home since I believe it might be my last for some time. I have a wonderful time with some of my friends and of course, Polly. She carries my barracks bag to the station to catch the train. You know – "little sis" has to be nice to her soldier "brother."

Just as soon as I arrive at SUI, I realize I am late with Polly's birthday card. I send her a card with a teddy bear making excuses for being late. To make the birthday card more personal, I find a place to write:

> Happy birthday and best wishes for a great year as an eighteen year old. (My, you are getting old.). May your school days become more enjoyable day by day. May you always have the ability to be useful and helpful to others. May you enjoy a long and healthful Christian life. In a few more years, may you find a fine husband, one that is intelligent, nice looking, religious, talented, and most of all true to you and worthy of you.

The Lord continues to help me to accept the fact that I have no chance of being anything to Polly other than a good friend, although I feel at times I love her just as much as ever. If I am tempted to dream of anything else, the information I receive while at home quickly shatters such dreams. Polly receives for Christmas a beautiful dresser set from Tom, engraved with his army insignia. But the thing that she really appreciates is an 8 x 10 picture of Tom. She is overjoyed when the picture arrives. He is truly a handsome soldier.

I receive a letter from Polly thanking me for the birthday card and especially for the "wax"(chewing gum) that I enclosed. It is difficult to purchase wax anywhere except at an army P.X.

> Really, honest Indian, I started writing you a week ago Sunday night and just have not finished it. The birthday card was just like you – don't get me wrong – I don't mean

you look like a teddy bear. Before I read the footnote saying not to let anyone read the poem, I had already read it
in the presence of a half dozen gaping females. Anyway, I
think it would have been a crime to have kept anything so
clever all to myself. Your card was here to welcome me the
night I came back, and my roommate, Martha, was just
dying to know what was in the bulky envelope. Well, she
found out. Now I can't keep her out of my wax.

Then Polly makes excuses for going with me to catch the
train. It is a good thing I did not allow myself to even dream
that there was anything unusual about this situation except a
big brother relationship. Otherwise I would have been terribly disappointed with her letter:

> I just want to say that you must have thought me a
> terrible impostor to bust in just when you were having
> your last minutes with your folks, and then to follow you
> to the train just like Mary and her lamb. Ha. But it had
> seemed so comfortable, like having part of the old gang
> back for a while, that I just hated to see it all dissolve
> again.

At the end of each quarter at SUI, I have been granted a
furlough. I am certain that I will get a few days leave on my
way to San Antonio, Texas, where I will (hopefully) be assigned to pilot training. So in my next letter to Polly, I ask for
a date during this leave.

I hope to accomplish two things on this date. First, I want
to find a way to end the "little sister" relationship with Polly.
I do not mind Polly using the "friend- neighbor" relationship

if she needs something to explain activities to Tom, but "little sister" is just too much. I reason she cannot call me "big brother" if she has a date with me.

Secondly, I want to be alone with Polly to see if she notes any changes in my personality. I feel that I am actually a new person (especially with girls) after the year at SUI. If she does not notice any changes, I will be terribly disappointed.

I grin as I remember, "I have known Polly for eight years and have been in love with her for over five years; I saw her just about daily for many years; I have been at countless parties with her; but this would be our first date if she accepts."

Polly answers my letter immediately. She will not get back on campus from her music tour for the college until Thursday. She knows she cannot get excused from Saturday morning classes. However, she will leave immediately after her last class and get home about 3:30 p.m., Saturday. She will have to return Sunday afternoon.

Well, one thing for certain, you can't second-guess the army. Since there are only five of us going to San Antonio, I am certain I will get a short leave on the way. No such luck! The complete Iowa City Company is transferred by troop train to Kansas City. I have to contact Polly in a hurry to cancel my date:

> Since I am to leave on a troop train at 6:00 this afternoon, I suppose I won't be able to celebrate the "Army Air Corps" with you. I could tell you how sad I am that I am not getting a furlough, but that would contradict my statement to you that I am never sad. I am sending this Special Delivery, Air Mail because I want it to reach you before Saturday. Thanks a lot for the letter. I realize you are very busy. Well, as I have to board the train in a few minutes, I will close and give this letter to the porter to mail.
>
> Buddy

The Uncertainty Of Life

I have no idea of my overall academic average at the State University of Iowa. I had a great deal of difficulty during the first quarter. However, during the last quarter, I have been solving the hard problems along with the outstanding cadets in the program. I am pleased with the final report placed in my service record. Perhaps, if I had known how much difficulty this short recommendation would cause me later, I would not have been so pleased.

To Whom It May Concern: Cadet Buddy Baskins was graduated from the Meteorology Unit at the University of Iowa, March 11, 1944. He was an excellent student on the basis of the following rating of superior, *excellent*, average, and unsatisfactory.

As I leave Iowa City I feel this has also been a great year for me socially. If there were any way to measure my development in this area, the rating would probably be *excellent* also.

I am no longer shy in the presence of prospective dates. In fact, I might have a bit too much confidence in myself with the opposite sex. No, I have not been able to get Polly out of my life completely. For example, the following comment is made by one of my friends in our yearbook at SUI:

> To one of the best pals I ever had. It has been a pleasure to share my secrets, my dates, and my car with you the past year. Will you ever forget Cedar Rapids? Remember the night when ten of us slept in the same room? Remember when you let us meet Lori for the first time? Say, now that you are leaving how did you manage to make a hit with such a wonderful girl? Then remember the time we told of the girls we had liked? I told about falling for my schoolteacher who was ten years older than I. You told of the only girl that had upset your life. I laughed at the crazy things you did. I said, "She must have been a swell girl to dent that hard heart of yours." You replied, "The world is full of swell girls."

Yes, I talk a big game, but I am well aware that there may never be another girl like Polly in my life.

As I ride the train to my next destination, San Antonio, Texas, I am fully aware that I am entering a period of uncertainty in my life. One does not make decisions in the army. The army makes them for you. I will be taking all kinds of tests, mental and physical, at the classification center. I have an eye stigmatism. Could this disqualify me for pilot training? Maybe I should have selected a research program along with some of my friends. Who knows what is best? But I am ready to help in the effort to win the war and at the same time to do something that will make Polly proud of me. So here goes.

Letter to Polly, San Antonio, March 23, 1944. To my surprise I am now a Lone Star State soldier. At the classification center, cadets are called "mister." Just imagine, "Mister Baskins." Also instead of calling us bad names, our officers call us gentlemen. I like everything fine except eating with one hand on the table and the other one below the table. I ruined both of my uniforms the first week, and still did not get enough to eat.

By the way, thanks for being patriotic and accepting my invitation for a date. It possibly was best that I did not get a furlough. You certainly would have been surprised when you saw me with my new root-a-toot burr haircut. You might have started running in the opposite direction crying, "What's that?" "What's that?" Of course, my good ma would have told you later that I was her son and not a stray monkey from the zoo.

Prior to the classification tests at San Antonio, our small group from SUI, who want to be pilots, agree that we can not do too well on the mathematics part of the tests, or we will be classified as navigators. So we purposely miss several mathematics problems and try to do exceptionally well on the parts relating to pilot training. Then comes the big day when we meet individually with the classification officer. "Cadet Baskins," he says, "It seems you did not do too well on the mathematics part of this test."

"Yes sir."

"That seems strange. Your record states that you studied a year of higher mathematics at the State University of Iowa. Your commander attached a letter that your work there was excellent. Doesn't that seem strange to you, *Mr. Navigator.*"

We didn't have a chance at being pilots.

My next letter from Polly indicates how time changes everything. In a short seven months, Polly changes from a homesick beginning freshman in college to a happy college co-ed with concerns about how she will survive the summer without the fellowship of the college gang. Then she tells me about Tom's furlough. She comments it was wonderful having him home even if she could be with him only on weekends. She had expected him to be changed a lot, but except for the fact he seems more serious-minded, he is just the same.

I have wondered for two months why Polly was not writing. She explains everything in her letter. When she is serious with Tom, she stops writing to me. Too bad I did not get that date in March. Maybe then she would not feel obligated to tell her big brother about the two weekends with her boyfriend.

Before navigation school, we are required to become proficient in using a fifty-caliber machine gun mounted in an airplane. So it is off to gunnery school at Brownsville, Texas. At Brownsville, it is hot, humid, and terrible. There are big mosquitoes everywhere. There is no way I can get a good night's sleep because of the mosquitoes. I finally decide that sweating all night is better than being eaten alive by mosquitoes, so I cover all of my body except my mouth and nose with a sheet. How the mosquitoes get under the sheet I will never know. Another problem is my fair skin, especially my nose, which blisters in the Texas sun. Finally, I create a small paper tent to tape over my poor nose.

Our first training at gunnery school involves standing in the back of a truck, which is moving down a skeet range at twenty miles an hour. We are target practicing with an automatic shotgun. Supposedly, this is to teach us that our motion makes a difference in hitting the "birdie."

The second phase of our training involves shooting fifty caliber machine guns on a practice range. We learn how to thread the cartridges into a tape and insert the tape into the gun. On the range, we shoot at moving targets. You can really tear up a target with these babies, if you can hit it. Then we are taught all about parachutes. Floating through the air under a parachute sounds so great it makes a fellow long some day for the words, "bail out."

Finally we are introduced to our first airplane, a worn-out B-24. It looks to me like a bull with a forked tail or maybe two tails. It has a wart on its bottom and a wart on its top. It stirs up dust with four nostrils, called engines. I am in the air force and have never been in an airplane of any kind. Will I like flying? I think so. The pilots of the B-24s are "slap-happy" fighter pilots who have completed their tours of combat duty. They try to fly the B-24s as if they are fighter planes. They often take a container of some kind of alcoholic beverage on a flight. Some are half-drunk before landing. To say they are unhappy at flying B-24s would be the understatement of the day. It is good that I do not know of the high accident rate at this base until I have completed my gunnery training. Otherwise, I would have been scared of flying in worn-out B-24s with crazy pilots.

Then comes the big day, the day I will fly in a plane and shoot a machine gun at targets. About an hour before take-off time, I pick up my equipment. First, I am given a parachute and harness. Then I receive communication equipment. I understand the need for earphones, but the leather strap that contains two things that look like half hickory nuts baffles me. "This is your microphone," explains the sergeant. "Strap this tightly around your neck with a microphone on each side of your Adam's apple." I say to myself, "He's crazy, if he thinks I talk through my Adam's apple." The last item is a wooden box full of cartridges. Boy, is it heavy!

We carry all of our equipment to our bull (B-24), and the co-pilot gives us our instructions. "Baskins, go to the tail turret. Load your ammunition and plug in your communication equipment. Then wait for instructions from the pilot." In a few minutes I hear, "Pilot to Baskins. Do you hear me? Over." I reply, "Baskins, reporting. I hear you loud and clear. Over." "Good. Unhook your communication equipment, and bring your parachute to the front for take-off." That old bull really stirs up the dust as we leave the runway. I am glad I have on earphones because the noise is as loud as a threshing machine.

Here I am in the tail turret of a B-24 flying about fifty feet above the water on a target range in the Gulf of Mexico. In addition I am talking through "hickory nuts" on my Adam's apple. I sound pretty good. It is hot in the tail turret, and the tail end of the plane is going up and down ten feet per second. This action is just like a stomach pump. In addition, the smoke from the shells fills the turret, and I become deathly sick.

I learn my lesson the first day. We carry our ammunition onto the plane in wooden boxes. After the first day, I immediately load all of my ammunition in the gun, even though the turret becomes crowded. Then when the action starts, I have the wooden box for my sickness. I have to scrub the turret only after the first flight. It is easy to carry the box off the plane. Somewhat smelly, but easy.

Do I get scared during my first airplane flight? Not really! Maybe I am too sick to think about being scared, but I am literally frightened to death during my third flight. We are flying over the target range, and discover a fisherman in a small boat on the edge of the range. The pilot contacts the control tower and asks permission to go ahead and fire at the targets. The control tower responds, "You know the regulations. You are not to use the target range if there is anyone in any part of it." Instead, we have to go to a second target range some distance away and wait our turn to get on the range. Our pilot is angry. "Pilot to crew. We're going down and teach that fisherman a lesson. This is the third day he has been on my target range." The lumbering B-24, trying to act like a fighter plane, dives for the small boat. The fisherman jumps into the water. The B-24 heads up immediately, and the wash from the engines topples the boat. "Pilot to Baskins. What do you see? Over."

"Baskins to pilot. I'm glad to report that the tail of the plane did not touch the water. We were very close, maybe a foot from the water." (I was scared beyond description. We were twelve inches from death. If the sea had caught the tail of the plane, we would have been goners.)

"I don't care about that. What about the boat?"

"The boat is floating upside down. The fisherman is in the water. The fisherman is shaking his fist at us. Over."

"Great. Maybe that fisherman will stay off the range, now. Over and out."

Finally, the suffering ends, and in early September we begin our training to become navigators at Hondo, Texas. I would have preferred any other navigation school because Hondo is near San Antonio, Texas. We have been told that

San Antonio has more soldiers per capita than any city in the United States.

The day we enter navigation school our pay increases by fifty percent. It is called flight pay. This is great. Also, we have rooms in which to live rather than open barracks. My roommate, Jimmy Waters, a good-looking cadet with black curly hair, is from Boston. He becomes my best friend in the air force. There is nothing unusual about navigation school. After a few weeks of preliminary study, our routine becomes one day in the classroom and the next day in a small plane where we practice our skills with several cadets working at separate tables. The nice thing about navigation school is that there are no classes on Saturday, so we go into San Antonio and try to have a good time. What a terrible city for a soldier!

Up to this time, I purposely have not dated anyone regularly because I know as a soldier I will be staying only a short time at any one place. Also I have no desire for any relationship beyond friendship. I guess my one love is still Polly. Since I am to be in navigation school for several months, and since I need dates occasionally to keep Polly off my mind, I decide that maybe I should try to find a steady. Since San Antonio is completely saturated with soldiers, it is not a good place to search. I tease about this situation in a letter to Polly.

> In San Antonio, there are thirty soldiers for every available girl. Every GI tries to get himself a steady girl because if you go to town without a definite date to receive you, you might as well reconcile yourself to walking on the streets until the M.P.'s chase you back to camp.
>
> I too tried to get a girl. For weeks I had no success. I did not even get to say hello to a girl. Then one weekend I met someone at a dance. Her name was Agnes.

Agnes and I got along great. So well, in fact, that before the weekend was over I asked her to be my steady girl.

"Of course," she said.

I pinched myself with joy. "You really mean it?" I asked.

She smiled sweetly, "Of course, honey."

"Now that we are going steady," I said. "I'll see you every time I get into town."

She touched my hand gently. "Yes," she whispered.

The next weekend I was in town and phoned Agnes. Her mother said she was at the dance. I went to the dance, and as I started to enter I saw Agnes coming out with a soldier on each arm.

"Hey, Agnes," I called.

"Hello Sam," she said.

"My name is Buddy," I corrected.

"Oh honey," she laughed, going away. "I forgot. There are so many of you."

I try every trick I learned at SUI in an attempt to locate a satisfactory date, but none of my "training" seems to work in San Antonio. The girls I want to date simply do not date soldiers. The fact that I finally find a steady that I like and enjoy in San Antonio happens by accident. I am in a department store for the purpose of purchasing some handkerchiefs. I never have enough. Mine seem to walk away. Finally, I find some, but to pay for them, I have to stand in line behind several other customers. When I get close enough to see the clerk, she is young and very pretty, with a winsome smile. I quickly observe that she is not wearing a ring. Before paying for the handkerchiefs I remark, "You are an outstanding clerk."

"Is that so? Why?"

"A lot of reasons, but number one is enthusiasm. Have dinner with me after you get off from work, and I will tell you the other reasons."

"I do not date soldiers."

This is just the challenge I need. If she does not date soldiers, she probably is the kind of girl I am seeking in my desire to date someone regularly. I look at several items in the store with no intention of purchasing anything. I finally find a time she is not busy.

"Hi, I'm here again. Would you call having dinner with someone dating? Surely eating a few bites across the table from someone would not be called a date."

A customer is approaching her table. "Let me think about it for a few minutes. Are you a nice person?"

I say "Yes" with a big smile as I slip away and wait for my next chance to be alone with her. There is no time for chatting, but between customers I get the message I want to hear. "I'll see you at the front door at 7:00."

She bursts through the front door loaded with assertions. The main one is that she has to go home immediately after the dinner. The second one is that I cannot take her home. Since my main objective is to cultivate her friendship, I take these assertions as part of the game.

In less than ten minutes she is talking up a storm, and enjoying it. I do not take her home, but we certainly have a long dinner. I learn a lot this first evening with her. She has just graduated from high school, and only recently started working at the department store. She does not know her plans concerning college. At this time she does not have a steady boyfriend. She is a Christian with high moral standards, attending mass every week. Finally, I get what I have been working toward all evening, her telephone number and extension at the department store. As she boards the bus to go home, my last words are, "I'll call you about dinner next Saturday night."

Her reply is, "You soldiers always say that."

I have dinner, but not a date, with Marie the next Saturday night. We must have walked five miles in San Antonio before I escort her to the bus again. We could not find a stopping place in our talking. One thing is obvious. We enjoy being together. I am not the typical soldier wolf she had expected. And I am pleased that she has high moral standards and does not smoke. The third weekend I do not invite her to have dinner with me. I ask her for a date, which could include dinner if she wishes. Of course, on a date I will enjoy holding her hand as we walk toward her home.

Yes, I find my steady in San Antonio. We are together just about every Saturday night until I finish navigation school. Sometimes we go to places that cater to high school youngsters; other times we go to a movie. Occasionally we eat at one of the fancy places in San Antonio. I run around with my cadet friends Saturday afternoon and have a date with Marie Saturday night. (She does not get off work until 7:00 p.m.)

Why do I date Marie just about every Saturday night until I leave navigation school? Apart from the fact that I like her, I want to try "going steady." Perhaps this is just what I need to forget Polly. Also, dating Marie is good for my ego. When she decides to "dress up," some cadets would call Marie beautiful. I can imagine hearing them say, "Where did that ugly cadet get that beautiful girl?"

Does having a steady help me to forget Polly? It may have helped a bit but not very much. With time I long to be transferred from San Antonio. Going steady simply has not worked. I am afraid Marie will get serious. I have no desire to be attached to anyone when I am on my way to combat, and there is always the chance that I will not be returning. But the real problem is that I have never found anyone who compares well with Polly. Marie is such a kind, sweet person; I do not want to hurt her in any way. So I wait for the army to do my dirty work for me. They transfer me from San Antonio. Marie does not enjoy writing letters; so soon we lose all contact with each other.

As I approach the end of my navigation training, three truths clutter my thinking process. I expect to be in combat soon. I want duty in Europe because I feel that the war will terminate there sooner than in the Pacific. My main desire is to get combat behind me. When I read of the escalating casualty rate for the air force in Europe, I must admit that this gets my attention.

Then the bottom drops out of my life. I receive a letter from Rocky Hill containing the rumor that Polly and Tom are engaged. I realize anew that for five years I have been in love with Polly. I also remember that in this five-year period she seemed to prefer Tom. This engagement is not something I had not expected. I have known for some time that Tom is crazy about Polly. However, this knowledge still knocks me for a loop. Immediately, there seems to be a big vacuum in my life. I wonder if I should stop corresponding with Polly. I do not want to do anything that might cause her difficulty. Before making any rash decisions, I feel I need additional information. To one friend I inquire, "How did you hear that Polly is engaged?" To another I ask, "Does Polly wear an engagement ring?"

I soon get a complete explanation of how the rumor started in Rocky Hill. Tom did indeed have a ring, and his younger sister saw it. She was so pleased she mentioned it to a high school friend who lived in Rocky Hill. This was the birth of the rumor.

Later I learn that Polly was not wearing a ring when she came home from college. I really do not know that Polly is engaged. All I know is the rumor that Tom had a ring. Maybe he did not purchase the ring. Maybe he took it back to the jewelry store. Maybe Polly would not accept the ring, and he still has it.

Soon after Christmas I will be finishing navigation school. It will take just a few weeks to get acclimated to a new plane and a crew, and then I will be ready for combat. I want to complete my combat missions as soon as possible, get back to the States, and be ready to begin life as soon as the war ends.

Navigators who have flown the required number of missions in order to return to the States are replacing many of the instructors. One of my instructors, Ron Kitchens, is in this category. One day I see him at a table outside the P.X., trying to forget bad memories. "Can I join you, Captain Kitchens? I need to ask you some questions, in case I have an opportunity to select my plane for combat."

"Certainly. Just do not select B-17s."

"Why is that?" I ask.

"In all my first missions as a navigator on B-17s, every effort was made on bombing missions to protect the planes and the crews. Also, we were able to complete our tour of duty in twenty-five missions. All that has changed."

"Why?" I ask.

"Let me explain with an example involving the infantry. Sometimes a heavily armed town occupied by the enemy is blocking progress of the United States Army. The town must be taken. A company is assigned the responsibility of taking this town. To accomplish this goal will require heavy casualties for this unit. However, this company is expendable for the overall good of the army. In this war, flights of B-17s represent this expendable company. Massive formations of B-17s are flying every day over Germany without adequate fighter protection, into heavy flak areas in open daylight. With so many planes in the air, some are bound to get through to the target. We are losing a large number of B-17s each day, but for each B-17 shot down we are probably saving thousands of lives for those fighting on the ground. This massive bombing by B-17's is definitely shortening this war."

"It seems that the B-17s are doing a good job."

"Yes, but I would stay out of B-17s. It's like joining a suicide squadron. Under the present circumstances of having to complete thirty-five missions before being relieved, I figure that less than fifteen percent of the flying personnel will accumulate enough missions to come home before being shot down. I thought I was not going to make it, and I did not have many missions to fly under these circumstances."

"Thank you, captain. It was really good to talk to you. I must get to class."

If I have a choice, I am thinking about selecting B-17s. This seems the only way to get to the European theater. I want to get into action and get my combat duty behind me. If I have to fight, I would just as soon fight every day, as opposed to fighting periodically over many months. However, the fifteen percent who make it through a tour of duty (or the eighty-five percent who do not make it) stays on my mind as

I pray each night. Yes, I am ready to go. I will be in the fifteen percent who complete all missions safely. I do worry about the sadness of my family if I am wrong. Also, I wonder if Polly will miss me.

Why should Polly's name come into my mind every time I am praying about serious matters such as how to face death courageously, if such is the will of God? Every time I pray, there is Polly. Has God's protection from my feelings for her lasted only two years? What does God expect of me?

After many hours of prayer, I seem to have the answer, but I am not happy with the answer. It seems that I am supposed to tell Polly of my feelings for her, not three years ago, but my feelings today. The very idea! She is probably engaged. She does not want to hear this from me, and I do not want to be embarrassed. Finally, the answer to my prayers seems a bit better. I am not to tell of my feelings for her until I leave the States for combat. Does this mean that I will not return?

Is Polly Really Engaged?

Well, the army has a way of doing things just opposite to that expected. I believe I am within a few days of being on my way to my final training in preparation for combat. I am ready both mentally and physically to accomplish great feats to impress Polly. But the army has other plans. Replacements, who are completing duty assignments in Europe, have not arrived to become instructors in the navigation school. The four students with the highest grades in the graduating class are selected to become temporary navigation instructors. How unlucky can you get? My roommate and I are two of the four.

The only good part of my new assignment is a fifteen-day furlough immediately after graduation. Polly is back in school. I want to see her. Maybe I will go to Campbellsville. I really need to know whether she is wearing an engagement ring in college. Also I need to begin preparing her for the letter I am going to write as I leave for combat. As I write her on Christmas day, I note it has been about a year since I last saw her. I have not written her for several weeks. I do not tell her it is because I have been trying to learn whether or not she is engaged.

(Hondo Air Force Base, December 25, 1944) O.K. I admit it. I did wait a long time before answering your letter, but "honest" I have been rushed practically to death the past few days. We have been flying day and night making long hops in the afternoon and returning at night. We visited several cities, but we could not leave the airfields as we were dressed in our flying suits. You should see me in my sheepskin-flying suit. I look like a teddy bear.

Before I forget it, Merry Christmas and Happy New Year. As for Christmas here, I am catching up on much needed sleep. You don't know how much I wished to be home Christmas. I certainly missed the good times we have had in the past.

The guys in the next room are "trying on" their clothes (officer's uniforms) and discussing them. We have a little problem. The army gives you a list of the different articles an officer must have before he can get his commission. Then the army gives you only $250 to purchase new uniforms. No matter how hard you shop, you are not able to buy all you need for $250. So far, I have purchased the necessities with the exception of some type of overcoat. If you see a frozen cabbage head running around, you will know it is I.

I am hoping to get a furlough after graduation. I know you will be back at Campbellsville. I would like to see you. Don't be surprised to see me walking up the campus sidewalk some afternoon if you are allowed to have visitors during the evening on weekdays. If it is not okay for me to drop by, write your mother and have her tell me.

✧

I am the only passenger to get off the train in Rocky Hill. At first, no one recognizes me, since I am so "dressed up." Then someone shouts, "It's Buddy." Everyone is shaking my hand, patting me on the back, and giving me a visual inspection. They have not seen a soldier in a brand new uniform, and a fancy uniform at that. I wait a few minutes to get my baggage. Mom and Dad have already learned that I am in town, and they are on their way to meet me. We are really "hugging-it-up" when I see that a soldier is walking toward the depot. He gives me a sharp salute. I break away from the hugs, and return his salute with my air force special. Mom and Dad stand amazed. Finally, one of them asks, "Do all soldiers salute you?" "Enlisted men are supposed to," I reply. The glow on my father's face indicates how proud he is of "his" son. The fact that I am an officer does not seem to affect Mother a great deal, but Dad is very pleased. No soldier from Rocky Hill has become an officer in the army. He wants me at the store as much as possible to show off "his" son. Because of gas rationing, I do not know whether or not he has any gasoline, but when I ask about going to Campbellsville, he says "yes" in such a way that I know he would have given me his last drop of gasoline.

There is a short note for me at Rocky Hill from Polly. The note contains several reasons as to why I should not make the trip: new snow, slick roads, roads full of pot- holes, etc. My first thought is that she does not want me to come to Campbellsville. But then her last words are, "Sure hope I get to see you." All I need are these seven words. Tomorrow I will be on my way.

I have been taught that all air force officers should have plenty of self-confidence for emergencies. At this stage of my life I have more than my share of confidence. It is hard for me to realize that less than eighteen months ago I was a shy, bashful youngster. Not only do I feel self-assured, I am satisfied with the way I look. My new dress coat fits like a tailored uniform, and my flight jacket is perfect. My cap is cupped in just the right spots to show I am a dashing air force officer. In addition, I am making more money than I have ever made, with officer's pay and flying pay.

As I drive toward Campbellsville College, I make my plans to accomplish four goals. First, I want to learn whether or not Polly wears an engagement ring in Campbellsville. Also I hope to destroy the big brother image. Yes, I am selfish, but I want Polly to meet the new Buddy. And finally, of much more importance than the other three goals, it is important for Polly to get the impression that I might have an interest in her beyond being a next door neighbor, friend. I have to be very careful. I have no intention of causing difficulty if she is really engaged to Tom. Frankly, I am so fond of Polly that I do not trust myself. I keep reminding myself over and over that I am simply building the foundation to prepare her for the letter I will write when I leave for combat. That is all.

I arrive at mid-afternoon. It is a typical January day in Kentucky, a bit cloudy but no rain or snow. Polly has completed her classes. She may have had a work schedule, but this has been canceled. She takes one look at me, and I can tell she is pleasantly surprised. She starts planning how to "show-off" her visitor. She has some difficulty. It seems that I want to talk to each of her friends. Being sociable with ease has become my second nature.

The former pastor at Rocky Hill, whom I call Brother Pierce, has moved to a church near Campbellsville. In late afternoon, we decide to visit the Pierces. Polly's roommate, Martha, goes with us. This is great. The three of us sit on the front seat, and Polly is forced to sit close to me. It feels good! Then too, if it is known in Campbellsville that Polly is engaged, Martha's presence will dampen any possible criticism. The main reason I am pleased that Martha is with us involves my fear that I will say something to Polly I should not say. Immediately, Polly and Martha are enjoying themselves telling me about what is dear to their hearts, Campbellsville College. Sometimes, they are so excited they were talking at the same time.

The visit with the Pierces is tremendous. They insist that we stay for dinner. Brother Pierce is just as much a comedian as ever, and I seem to be in rare form. Sometimes Polly looks at me with the expression "Is this the Buddy Baskins I once knew?" We laugh and talk until we have to leave to get Polly and Martha in the dorm before the doors are locked.

On the way back to the dorm we note that the clouds have moved away so we stop at a roadside park, and the three of us enjoy God's creation in the heavens. The sky is filled with bright stars, which gives me the opportunity to show off my knowledge of astronomy by naming a few of them. Then Polly and Martha find one, which they name Maggie. She is supposed to be the girl that one day I will marry. Tonight, she takes on many undesirable traits, bestowed on her by my two companions.

Yes, it has been a great evening. I have accomplished all of my goals. It seems that Polly does not wear an engagement ring in Campbellsville. It is possible that her engagement is simply a rumor. When we arrive back at the dorm, there are a few minutes before "lock-up" time. Polly and I are alone in the car. I caution myself. Keep your feelings to yourself. Be careful what you say. "Whew! Only five minutes until lock-up time. Not much time to tell you what a terrific day this has been."

"Yes, it has been a great day. Thank you so much for making the long trip to Campbellsville. Thank you for being so nice to my friends."

"You have so many nice friends in Campbellsville, especially Martha."

"Yes, Martha is a true friend. She has helped me grow as a Christian."

"Polly, Campbellsville has been good for you. I can't really describe it. You know I once thought that you were the cutest little girl I had ever seen. Now you are a lovely, sophisticated co-ed."

"You are the one who has really matured. I know a year is a long time, but you have changed so much. You have always had a good personality, but your personality now is so compelling everyone seems to enjoy being around you."

"I like you just the way you are now, Polly."

"Let's not change until we see each other again."

"Let's agree to never change."

"Okay."

"Polly, do you remember when I first fell for you as a cute twelve-year old girl? Later my love for you was so great I did not know what to do, so I made many mistakes. It took me a long time to get over this puppy love."

"You managed. I hear now you have a beautiful girl in every port."

"But if you were at my port, none of them would have a chance."

"You have a way of saying nice things."

"Time is just about up. I need one more close look at you, Polly. I may not see you again for three or four years. Yes, the mysterious twinkle is still there."

"What do you mean?"

"I mean the twinkle in your eyes. I have always been able to see it. I like to think it is there just for me. Don't lose that twinkle before I see you again."

At the door, which soon would be locked, I tell her again what a wonderful time I have had at Campbellsville. "Thank you for a perfect evening. Promise me, Polly, you won't lose that twinkle in your eyes. I'm going to call it, my twinkle. Promise!"

"If it's there, I promise. Goodnight and have a safe trip home."

I quickly return to the car without looking back. What I really want to do is to take her in my arms, and give her a kiss that will truly show my feelings for her. As I drive away I am grateful that I did not say or do anything that might be detrimental to Polly if it is true that she is engaged to Tom. At the same time I believe I have built a good foundation for the letter I will write on the way to combat.

When I arrive back at the air force base in Hondo, I immediately send her my address. I do not say in this letter what I want to say. I have to be careful. I worry that I said too much while at Campbellsville.

From Hondo, Texas, January, 1945. Just a few lines to let you know where I am stationed in case you should ever find time "heavy on your hands" and decide to write to the "old man" (what we are called since we have been made instructors.) Boy, oh boy, do I hate to start back to work after fifteen wonderful days (thanks to you and other friends), but tomorrow we start making plans for a new class of cadets. I don't know how long I will be here, but I imagine not very long as we are supposed to be replaced by those coming back from combat. I don't know why I am sending you my address for if you wait as long to write this time as we usually do, I'll be at another base. If you must know this is a hint that I long for a quick reply.

✧

Polly does not write immediately. However, the "second-hand" information I receive indicates my trip to Campbellsville accomplished my desired goals. It seems that Polly is really surprised at how charming I have become, in a strong gentlemanly sort of way. This is great. I did make an impression on her friends. I await her letter to see if my actions suggested that I might have some interest in her beyond the friend-neighbor status. This is important in preparation for the letter I will write soon. There is so much to accomplish in a short period of time that I determine not to become complacent. I send a five-pound box of candy for Valentine's Day. I also give her another hint as to my feelings for her by enclosing a copy of a poem with the candy.

Please Be My Valentine
May this show my appreciation for a very, very enjoyable evening at Campbellsville. May I also thank you for helping to make my last furlough one of my best furloughs. As you know, Polly, I have never been able to explain my actions; therefore, I won't try to explain my feelings, but maybe this little poem will partially show my appreciation in a true Valentine spirit.

It's not the life we airmen live,
It's not the love we have to give,
I know it's hard, but don't you see,
What just a memory means to me.

The war will end, we hope, someday,
And we, again, can have our way;
So here's a wish that, someday, you and I
Will meet again, and maybe "Give love a try."

I finally get a letter from Polly, dated February 14,1945. As usual, I am very impatient. However, the letter is so great that it makes me forget its lateness.

Actually, the letter contains few facts or definite statements. It does hint at many things. I have to remind myself to be rational and to analyze each statement very carefully. From the overall tone of the letter it is obvious that Polly knows I have an interest in her beyond the friend-neighbor relationship. In fact she seems to welcome this interest. Although I am very pleased with the letter, my mind is now filled with questions and thoughts:

I do not believe that Polly is engaged. I know her well and have complete trust in her. She would not have encouraged my interest in her if she were engaged. The rumor is false. I have no idea of the details, but Polly is not engaged.

I do not think I have to worry any more about the big brother, little sis titles. I have longed for a way to terminate this relationship, and thank goodness it has happened.

Did I accomplish the number one goal of my trip? Yes, it seems that I did. It will not be a shock to Polly when I write my letter on the way to combat.

Polly begins with the explanation that her letter will be void of foolishness and wisecracks, which usually characterize her letters. "This letter is from me –the real me." She expresses appreciation for the Valentine candy and adds, "The fact that it came from you is what counts. Buddy, please take this for what it is worth because I'm not saying it flippantly." She then states that there always seemed to be something that kept us from being the close friends we might have been. From the tone of her letter I know she does not mean next-door neighbor friends. She notes that when I was at home while Sis was on the mission field, this tenseness between us seemed to diminish. Then she writes:

> Buddy, when you came to Campbellsville – well, it's not necessary to tell you how it affected me because you could plainly see. Why, I was as excited as a sixteen year old. My, my, that was three years ago.

Sweet, sweet Polly – surely she must know the cause of the tenseness between us. I have loved her so much and yet have tried so hard to keep her from knowing the full extent of my love. I want to say to her, "With all the opportunities I have given you, you have never, until this letter, let me know you had any interest in me except as neighbor-friend or big brother." No, I won't tell her right now how much I love her, but I am expecting to tell her everything as I leave for combat. In the meantime, she will be getting so many hints that she will in no way doubt any part of my farewell letter. I will soon be on my way to combat, so I am going to enjoy every minute of letting her in on the big secret of my life, a little at a time—namely, I love her and have loved her for six years.

In her letter Polly says some things about me that I never expected to hear from her.

> Now, I am going to tell you a few things about yourself. You probably know it, but you have a charming personality, and no one can help liking you. You have an I.Q. that makes me squirm when a matter that requires intelligence is being discussed. Your looks are not half bad. (Gee, I'm getting fresh.) You have talent that can take you anywhere you want to go, if you just use it wisely and don't waste it.

Really, Buddy, I'm not kidding about any of this, and I guess it's crazy – my writing it – but I just suddenly wanted to tell you, and so I did.

Then she closes the letter with "Thanks for everything – even the poem, *It Isn't The Life We Airmen Live.*" Since the last two lines of the poem are:

So here's a wish that, someday, you and I
Will meet again, and maybe "Give love a try,"

I am certain that Polly has some interest in me beyond a next-door neighbor friendship. I certainly will investigate whether or not this intuition is true. In fact, Polly gives me just the opportunity I need. In the words of an old country saying, "She left a crack in the barn door," and I am going to slip in. Along with her compliments of me, she also talked about her own inadequacies. This provides excellent ammunition for my next letter.

Polly, you are the most modest girl in all the world, but I think you are wonderful. If you were in your clumsy mood while I was at Campbellsville, please don't change. Really though, I know you were not. If anyone was running around like a chicken with its head off, it was I, and honest, for a guy who is known to talk a lot but say little, I was wordless. I could think of nothing suitable to say as there was only one thought in my mind. I should not tell you this, but all I could think of was "taking you in my arms and giving you a big kiss." Isn't this a silly thing to say, but honest, it is the truth.

I wanted to tell you about all the ways that college had helped you to develop into a "superb young lady." You were once my ideal girl, and I wanted to tell you how glad I was that you had not changed too much, just the right amount. I finally said something about the twinkle in your eyes (and I can see it even if no one else can). In spite of all my blunders, I had a very, very enjoyable time at Campbellsville.

Polly, honest, I am really ashamed of you. The very idea of your saying there wasn't much about you to encourage friendship. My goodness! Most girls would give their eyeteeth to be in your shoes. You are the type of girl a guy dreams about. You are wonderful. Anyway, I cannot give a fair description of you, as I like you too much.

The next day. Polly, this is Wednesday morning, and right now I am debating whether or not to mail this letter. I am not certain I should tell you I like you very, very much (and not simply as a friend). You probably cannot make heads or tails of this letter so after the first page is read just fold and return. I don't want to cause trouble.

I realize after I mail the letter that I have said too much. Many things could have caused Polly to show, for the first time, an interest in me beyond friendship. Maybe she and Tom had had a quarrel, and this was her way of getting even with him. Maybe I went too far in trying to impress her friends. Anyway, the letter is in the mail, and it will serve as a stepping-stone to the letter I will write on my way to combat. Before my letter reaches Campbellsville, I receive a second letter from Polly. She explains that she has received a letter from her mother indicating that I have volunteered for the thrilling life of a B-17'er. She needs to remind me of something.

Buddy, don't forget at any hour of any day that your first love and duty is toward God – because after all – the fact that you've had all the good things you have had thus far have not been due to luck, have they?

Hondo, Texas, February 20, 1945. Yes, it is true that I volunteered for B-17s, but in the army that doesn't mean much. I may be assigned to B-24s or B-29s. Polly, I know you are praying for me, and I am very grateful. Yes, I pray for you just about every day. Keep praying for me; you are such a strong Christian. I just received word that I am on a shipping order to Lincoln, Nebraska, leaving here on Friday, March 1. I hope to spend one or two days at home during the weekend on the way to Lincoln. I would certainly like to see you, but I understand that this is a late notice, and you may have a full schedule for that weekend.

You have a crazy letter on the way to you. You may have already received it. If I said too much, please forgive me. I do not want to cause trouble. However, that does not erase the fact that I like and admire you very much.

I am able to stop by Rocky Hill to see my parents on Saturday and Sunday on my way to Lincoln, Nebraska. I am very disappointed. I was certain Polly would be there. I remember she found a way to be at home each time Tom was home on furlough. "Well, I guess this brings me back down to earth." I can hardly wait for the two days to end. Yes, I am heartbroken. I ask myself the question, "Why do I always strike out with Polly?"

I have not prayed for several months for the Lord to protect me from my feelings for Polly. I guess this prayer is still needed. When I arrive in Lincoln, I realize the Lord has answered my prayer. In our transfer to Lincoln, Nebraska, my good friend and roommate can not get all the way to Boston, Massachusetts and back to Lincoln in the time allowed, so he spends a few days in Omaha, Nebraska. In three days of leave, he finds his true love or so he claims. I arrive in Lincoln, tired and sleepy. I sit up most of the night listening to him talk about his new girl. "And you know, Buddy," he says. "She has a sister that behaves, acts, and thinks just like you. I have you set up for a date, Saturday night."

I am not very enthusiastic. I feel relieved that a "going steady" situation in San Antonio is over. Before my disappointing weekend, I start believing that things are improving with Polly. Evidently, it is just my imagination. I really do not want to cooperate with my roommate, but I do. Jimmy is right. Betty is different. Her humor, her energy, her pranks, her pleasing personality, her pleasant smile and her looks are just what I need to help relieve my anxiety over Polly and over the fact that I am heading for combat.

Soon two letters arrive from Polly via Hondo. She indicates she made every effort possible to get home but could not because of high water. The buses simply did not run. She too was disappointed because she kept thinking that maybe I would be able to get to Campbellsville. If I had received her letters before leaving, I probably would have headed for Campbellsville in spite of the high water.

The thing that thrills my heart is that Polly indicates she really wanted to see me that weekend. I have loved her for such a long period of time that it seems a miracle that she has any interest in me. Her second letter brings a big lump to my throat.

> Maybe, I'll never mail this – maybe I will, but I'm writing it for my own relief so I'll probably say anything. I never wanted so desperately to be home in all my life. I practically begged several to drive me home, but all had plans for the weekend.

I would like to have a day's talk with you, but it looks like that will have to wait a bit. I've been going in a daze and a whirl since I got your letter, but I won't try to answer it now.

The last two sentences of Polly's letter overpower my mind. I have to get to Campbellsville. I tip heavily one NCO who reluctantly gives me a three-day pass, and a bigger tip goes to the NCO who places my name on a flight from Lincoln to Louisville, Kentucky. I have to get to Campbellsville. I have no guarantee there will be a plane from Louisville back to Lincoln. If not, I will be AWOL. Sometimes, you have to live dangerously. Especially, when it concerns someone you love.

The trip to Campbellsville is wonderful. I arrive early in the afternoon and check in at the hotel. I know I will be too tired to drive back to Rocky Hill tonight. I had a difficult time catching a plane to Louisville. There were only two passengers on the plane. The plane was loaded with freight. Actually, I was up most of the night on the trip. From the airport I caught a bus downtown and then a bus to Rocky Hill. I am worn out, but today is going to be worth the effort. Dad is so great about letting me use his rationed gasoline. I think in the back of his mind he knows I am crazy about this girl.

When I arrive on campus it is a beautiful day with no clouds. Again, Polly is ready to show off her guest. A big softball game is in progress. Polly and I are encouraged to participate. I remove my coat, tie, and shirt, down to my clean (at least I hope) T-shirt, roll up the legs of my pants, and we are ready to play. It is a spirited game, and both Polly and I enjoy it very much. When I am not on the field, I am busy making friends. This is my second nature now, especially with girls. It is a great afternoon.

Yes, we eat dinner again at the Pierces. It is a short drive, but one loaded with action. I am crazy about Polly, but I am not certain how she feels about me. What should be my next step? She is sitting fairly close to the door, but her hand is about halfway across the seat. I reach across and take her hand and gradually pull her closer to me in the seat. It is the first time I have held hands with Polly. I am so in love that the feeling of just holding hands is even more than I imagined it could be. I hold her hands so long this night that they must have been sore the next day.

I am determined to get some information about Tom on this trip so I ask, "How's Tom." Polly refuses to talk about the subject. Instead she says, "He's fine, but let's talk about your letters." I want to say, "I could talk about our letters more realistically if I had some idea of your relationship with Tom." Before the trip I learned that Tom wired flowers for Valentine's Day from the hospital where he is stationed in France. If they had had a quarrel, it did not last long.

Polly interrupts my thinking with: "You wrote in one letter that you liked me very, very much, and in the very next letter you apologized for saying too much."

"I did not apologize for what I said. I wrote that if I had said too much, then I was sorry. Did I say too much for someone who is considered only as a next-door neighbor, friend?"

"You should have no fear or saying too much when you know you can take it back in the next letter."

I want to say I was just concerned about making inappropriate statements to someone who might be engaged. Wisely I keep my mouth shut, and we forget about Tom for the rest of the evening. Instead I ask, "Did I really say too much?"

With a big smile she answers, "Any girl would be pleased to receive those words from you. That is, if you really mean them. I bet you say similar words to all of your girl friends."

"Polly, I admit I have dated many different girls. They have made the horrible life in the army a bit more pleasant." I want to say they have helped me to forget that I am madly in love with you. Instead I add, "However, I have had no desire for a close relationship with any of them. I'm not corresponding with any girl at this time except you."

"Let's talk about us. Thank you for coming back to Campbellsville."

"It's great to be with you again, Polly. I enjoyed so very much my first trip to Campbellsville, and this one is even better."

"I wish we could see each other more often."

"So do I, but I guess it is impossible. I expect to leave the states in a few months."

"I'm going to really miss you, especially since we are just getting to know each other as adults."

"I'm still a little boy in adult clothes."

"I guess I am still a little girl."

"I guess that is the reason I like you so very much."

"If you really knew me, it might be different."

"I have known you for nine years, Polly. If I don't know you now, I will never know you."

"And you still like what you see."

I take both of her hands in mine and look again into her beautiful eyes. "Very, very much, Polly. You mean more to me than any girl I have ever known. Thank you for keeping my twinkle in your eyes."

"I'm glad. Maybe it will always be there for you."

Time passes so rapidly when you are with the one you love. It is time to leave. I do not attempt to kiss her goodnight or goodbye. Since my love for Polly is the real thing, I have decided the first time I kiss her will be when she acknowledges that she loves me. This first kiss will be an act of love. I

140 / Is Polly Really Engaged?

have little control over my emotions on this leave. I am certain by this time she is fully aware that I am crazy about her. This does not bother me a great deal because I will be sharing my feelings with her in a few weeks as I leave for combat. Yes, just being with and close to her is all I need. This has never been true for any other girl I have known. Undoubtedly this must be a characteristic of being in love. There is no question now that it was the real thing and not puppy love that happened to me when I was fourteen.

Although I am completely worn out and sleepy, the evening has been so exciting that I cannot sleep. I don't know what time I finally get to sleep, but it seems I have not slept long when I receive a 6:30 a. m. call from Polly. She is generous in her parting words before she has to get ready for breakfast and class. She encourages me when she states she has never had a more pleasing, exciting, and happy evening in her life and cannot find adequate words to express her appreciation for my efforts to be there. I am so sleepy; I must be careful. I am afraid I will tell her what she means to me. I don't want to cause problems.

The air force plane is not available in Louisville, and I have to ride a train back to Lincoln. During the last twelve hours of the trip I am A.W.O.L (my leave time has expired). Since I do not get off the train from Chicago to Lincoln, I have no difficulty. On base, some of my friends have managed to cover for me.

The train trip is not too bad. I am floating on air. There is nothing more exhilarating than being close to the one you love. Either Polly is the best actress I have ever dated, or she too experienced a wonderful evening. The first thing I want to do is write her, telling of the sacrifices I made to get to Campbellsville. I want her to know of the chances I took just to see her. I want her to know that the evening was so exciting that I could not sleep at all although I was tired and sleepy. I want her to know that I think she is wonderful. Do I dare write these things in my letter? Finally reason takes over, and I tear up the first letter.

Lincoln, Nebraska, March 19, 1945. I finally learned that I am not Superman. I missed my plane in Bowman Field and had to take a train back to Lincoln. By the time I got here, I had a nice fever due to what most people might call the flu. I have not been to see the doctor, but I have been in bed for two days. I am nearly well now, and tomorrow morning we will begin a ten-day training course that must be finished before we can leave this base.

Please understand that I meant every word I said to you while in Campbellsville. I must ask the question, "Is it appropriate for me to say some of the things I said to you?" For example, do you think it is appropriate for a guy to tell a girl, who thinks of him only as a good friend, that she is tops or number one on his list of girls? Now tell me the truth. Do you think this is appropriate? Well, I don't think it fair, your knowing it, but since you do, all I can say is "It is the honest truth."

You see my problem is that I dream too much. In my dreams you like me, so then it is appropriate for me to tell you the truth. I guess I do not have very good control over my imagination. Do I? Well, at least I have fun dreaming. I had better stop this letter before I say too much (for a friend). Really, I'm not angry at myself for telling you the things I did, but I don't trust myself when I am with you.

Polly answers my letter with a six-page letter, but doesn't answer my question until the last page. The answer is not what I am seeking. My status is still that of a good friend. However, I am building a good foundation for the letter I will write soon.

She begins her letter by saying if I had received all the letters she has started to me the past week I would be completely submerged. She implies there are so many things she wants to tell me. ("Somehow, she never gets around to telling me these things.") She does make me feel great with this explanation:

> It wasn't any mere chance that caused me to be up at 6:30 a.m. the morning you left Campbellsville. To be frank, I just hadn't slept. I was too excited, and there were so many thoughts running through my head. I have been feeding my vanity on the "manna" of the idea that you weren't able to sleep that night for the same reason that I could not sleep. The phone call was silly – but so am I, so I did it.

Then she tells of a conversation with a guy whom she describes as, "the one with the western drawl." He first asks, "Where's that good looking flying man you had up here, yesterday?" His final comment is, "You know, I really liked him. He's the first one of them fellows I've seen that had any common sense. Most of those air force men are just plum stuck up." Well, at least I have one friend at Campbellsville.

Then she gives me an important news item: Her mother and dad have just sold their house in Rocky Hill and are moving to Bowling Green. She expresses her sadness, concluding with the statement:

> There's one thing about it, Buddy, We'll never find neighbors that will mean as much to us as the Baskins family. I mean that from the depths of my heart. Oh doggone that lump in my throat. I've got to change the subject.

Finally Polly answers the question I posed in the last letter.

Buddy, you paid me a higher compliment than you'll ever know the other night. In your letter you asked me if I really thought it appropriate for you to tell me what you did. I can't and must not tell you any more than this – your previous letter, your coming, and what you told me upset me more than anything I can remember. That's being frank, but I have given up pretenses. I haven't had a completely peaceful moment since, and as yet I can't explain why. As it is, for the time being I will just have to fight things through. But as for what you said being appropriate – is it customary for things along that subject to be appropriate?

Living By Faith

The long cold nights in the barracks at Lincoln, Nebraska provide plenty of time for deep and disturbing thoughts: "Well, I have done it again. I have allowed my love for Polly to take over my life just as it did a few years ago. I had great expectations that Polly's letters would indicate an interest in a closer relationship. This has not occurred. The big change is that she does write more often. For this I am grateful."

It seems I have but one recourse. I know that God arranged my wonderful visits to Campbellsville. Maybe the only reason for these visits was preparation for the letter I will write on the way to combat. I simply have no way of knowing. So I will do the only thing I know to do. I will turn everything over to the Lord.

If it is God's will for Polly to have an increased interest in me, He will keep the fire burning in her heart until I can see her again, even if it is months and months away. If not, He will protect me from my feelings for her as He has done in the past. In my letters I will continue to indicate my feelings for her, and let God take care of the rest.

Lincoln, Nebraska, March, 1945. Believe it or not I just got out of bed fifteen minutes ago, 8:55 a.m. to be exact. What a life! All we have been doing for the past week is signing a roll sheet at 9:00 a.m. So now you know why I got up at 8:55. I guess I would go back to bed if I thought I could sleep, but I have so many things I want to tell you I had better start your letter right now. I don't know why I am writing this letter today, because I know I will not mail it until I get to my new base, Sioux City, Iowa. We are due to leave Thursday night if the orders are not changed.

I very much want a picture of you, if you have one to spare. I really do not need a picture to see you for, as I have told you before, half of my time is spent dreaming of you. You mean more to me than a good friend in my dreams.

I would like to see you again soon, but I'm afraid such will not be possible. Let me repeat. I meant everything I said while I was in Campbellsville.

I do not have time to worry about Polly. The air force keeps me working day and night. My request has been granted. I am now a member of a B-17 crew, preparing for combat. The B-17 is a beautiful, graceful plane. There is one big problem. It is very slow in comparison to B-29s. Thus it is somewhat of a "sitting duck" for anti- aircraft guns and fighter planes. The navigator's work area is located in the nose of the plane, close to the bombardier. The view of the ground on cloudless days is wonderful, but there seems to be little protection in time of battle. The weather is cold on the ground in Sioux City, Iowa. In the air, we usually encounter thirty to forty degrees below zero weather. Thanks to the miracle of wool, we do not get cold. Before each flight we slip the sheep skin coveralls over our regular clothes; then the sheepskin jacket overlaps the overalls. The long sheepskin gloves overlap the sleeves of the coat. Then with the oxygen mask and the sheepskin cap over most of our head, there is not much left to get cold.

When I am not flying, I am checking my mail to see if I have a letter from Polly. Here is the answer I receive relative to my request for a picture.

> I don't have any pictures at present, and anyway it would depreciate too much in the company of all the pictures of other girls. But if I had one, I would send it to you. (By the way, what does Emily Post say about who sends whom a picture first? You see, I abide by her strictly.)

She concludes her letter with, "Still doing a lot of thinking." I interpret this to mean she is not yet ready to terminate our relationship (whatever it is). I'll keep sharing my feelings with her even if I get little response. I don't want the letter I will write on the way to combat to be too big of a surprise.

> **Sioux City, Iowa, April 1, 1945.** Right now I am very sleepy. Don't tell me I should stay home at night. I went to bed last night at 7:00 p.m. The rules say you are supposed to get eight hours of sleep before each flying mission to prevent carelessness and accidents. So at 7:00, like a good little boy, I climb into my comfortable sack (army nickname for bed). I could not go to sleep. I thought of a million things, a few of them simple thoughts, but

mostly fantastic dreams. I keep telling myself to stop dreaming, but I don't really want to stop because it is very nice having you like me more than a friend in my dreams.

It was really late before I got to sleep and did I feel terrible when I had to get up at 3:00 a.m. I guess I will get used to early hours, as we will get up at 3:00 every day that we fly, and we will fly every other day. I'll tell you one thing. Bacon and eggs do not taste good at 3:30 a.m. What makes it even worse is that today is Easter.

Tuesday: Boy, oh boy, what a day! I am in a bad humor tonight. I have a good reason. We were supposed to fly today, but when I looked out the window this morning (3:00 a.m.), it was snowing so hard you could barely see ten feet in front of you. Since we were not able to fly, we took a stiff medical examination instead. This would not have been so bad except they discovered my shot records were missing. Right now I have cholera, typhus, and smallpox in my right arm and tetanus, typhoid, and yellow fever in my left arm. Can you blame me for writing this letter in the middle of my sack? These shots are not supposed to bother you if you do not need them. I'm certain I took all of these shots last year, but I don't feel good. I think they gave me too many at one time.

Polly answers my letter ten days after I mail her letter. First she tells me the college news and then about her practice teaching. Finally she talks about some things that are on her heart. However, she does not mention Tom. I like to feel that this is progress, slow progress, but progress. I hope I am not wrong.

There are only thirty-seven more days until I leave Campbellsville College for good, and I like it better every day. I'll always be thankful I came here. I've come to know myself better here than ever before, and I'm much surer of myself and so much happier. I don't know whether you can tell it or not, but I know it within me. What I can't understand is why I write things like this to you?

Sioux City, Iowa, April, 1945. As usual we got up at 3:00 a.m. yesterday morning and worked very hard until we "made like a bird." We landed at 1:15 P.M. and guess what? I had to be at the hospital at 2:00 P.M. for a dental appointment. I finally got out of my heavy flying clothes and rushed to the hospital only to have to wait in line quite a while, and all because of one little tooth that ate too much candy and cake. Boy, was I hungry when we landed, but I waited until after my dental appointment. Then I was so hungry that I ate far too much. When I got back to my nice warm room, I fell asleep.

I guess this is enough about my troubles. Don't you get tired of hearing my troubles all of the time? Well, I have to tell my troubles to someone – troubles such as the fact that I have not received a letter from you for nearly two weeks. Really I am not like the soldier who received the Congressional Medal of Honor. A few weeks later the general asked him what his wife thought of the decoration. "Sir," said the soldier. "She doesn't know I got it yet. It isn't my turn to write." I'm really not that way, honest. I just can't think of anything to write until I get a letter from you.

You might be angry with me, and who knows you might have decided to scratch me out of your scrapbook. You said in the last letter "still thinking." But how am I to know if it is "good thinking" or "bad thinking"? It is easy for imaginations to run wild here, so I hope you are just too busy to write.

In Polly's next letter she pretends I have received the Congressional Medal of Honor from the joke I sent her. Then she explains that Martha dared her to give me a hard time. She is very excited about the May Day Festival. She and Martha are among the attendants of the May Day King and Queen. Also, she is playing the part of Dinah in the operetta, "The Ghost of Lollypop Bay," singing two solos. She does a good job of describing how she will have to rush behind stage, change from her formal into makeup, play the part of Dinah, scrub her face, jump back into her blue formal and march decorously back out in the recessional. I feel I am at Campbellsville for the festival. She closes the letter with a scripture verse.

> I'm not angry, and I certainly have not crossed you out of my scrapbook, you nut. That is not where I keep you. I only keep scraps there. Goodnight and good luck,
> Philippians 1:3,
> Polly

Sometimes I have Polly on my mind so much I forget I am in the air force. Then something happens to bring me back to reality. One day we are scheduled to give the bombardier some practice dropping bombs, so we head for the practice range. I call the pilot and inquire if he wants a heading to the practice range. His reply is, "What do you think I am, a nincompoop? As many times as we have been on this range, I could fly there with my eyes closed. You are excused from navigation duties today. I have another job for you. After we land it usually takes me half an hour to write up the report of our bombing practice. I want you to write the report as it happens and have it ready for me to sign as we leave the plane. The tail gunner will help you assess each bomb dropped. I would appreciate this very much."

I take the pilot at his word and pay little attention to maps until I hear the pilot say "We are approaching the first target. Bombardier, get ready to take over." Something just does not seem right so I start studying maps and the lay out of the target range. Then I hear, "Bombardier taking over." A bomb is dropped, and I quickly get in position to see where it lands relative to the target.

"Pilot to Navigator. How close did we come to the target?"

"We had a direct hit, sir."

"Great."

"I'm not certain."

"Why not?"

"I think that target was in a field on the Joe Jaggers farm."

"Oh no! What do you think we bombed?"

"I believe we had a direct hit on a haystack."

"Come in, tail gunner. Give me a report."

"I see dust in the air and a lot of small particles that could be pieces of hay."

"Let's get out of here. I'm turning ninety degrees to the left. Navigator, give us a heading to the next target."

I know the pilot is worried about what I will say in my write-up of our bombing of a haystack. I have been careful on all of my practice navigation flights to enumerate all of my mistakes. In fact, the pilot once said to me, "Baskins, you will never get promoted if you keep listing all of your mistakes." The pilot can wait no longer. "Baskins, how are you going to write this incident in the report."

"I've already written this part of the report."

"Let's hear it."

"We had a direct hit on the target selected."

"Good report, Baskins."

The crew teases the pilot by saying he is a hotshot navigator. They are always saying, "Let's go bomb a haystack." The pilot's willingness to let the crew tease him is a big boost to the morale of Crew 116, but not as much as another practice mission.

We are flying at a high altitude above the clouds and some distance from the base to give me some practice using celestial navigation. When we return to the base, we are in for a big surprise. The base is closed. An unexpected snowstorm has moved into the area, and the snow is so heavy we cannot land. We are advised to go south as rapidly as possible to try to get ahead of the storm. We head for the municipal airport at Des Moines, Iowa.

We finally make contact with the airport at Des Moines and receive the bad news that the blizzard has already reached the city, all power is off, and the airport is closed. We inform the airport that we have no choice but to land. Our supply of gasoline is just about gone. The airport is operating on an emergency power unit, but promises to turn on the runway lights at our request.

The pilot outlines for the crew the seriousness of the situation. "We probably have enough gasoline to make one attempt at landing. Visibility is just about nil. If we do not find a runway on this one attempt, we will use the remaining gasoline to attain as much altitude as possible before bailout. We will donate the plane to some Iowa cornfield. You have two orders at this time. First, stay off the communication system unless there is an emergency. This will be reserved for the copilot and navigator. Secondly, all except the copilot and navigator will attach their parachutes now for an immediate jump if such is necessary."

Then he gives instructions to the copilot and to me. "I am flying straight toward radio station WRAS in Des Moines.

Baskins, study the runways at the airport and select one we might use with a turn from our present direction. Then figure the angle of turn. Copilot, the navigator will give you the wind data and the angle of turn, and you will determine how far from the vertex we need to start the turn. Give this information to the navigator." "Baskins, you and I both know for this plan to work we must have accuracy greater than the manuals say is possible. Check, double check, and triple check our positions obtained from four or five radio stations. The time to turn must be one hundred percent accurate if we have any chance of finding the runway. Good-luck."

It is a terrible ordeal. We will be about a hundred feet above the tallest building in Des Moines before making our turn for descent to the field. I pray that our instruments are accurate. Otherwise we might crash into a building.

The high wind does not seem to be changing very much. For four radio stations in a row our airspeed remains constant. If this continues, we might have a chance of finding a runway. For the last radio station there is a drastic change. A decision has to be made immediately. There is no time to think about the problem. Should I use the data that remained constant through four radio stations, or should I use the last information? The wrong decision will mean we will miss the runway. There is no time left. I decide we are entering a part of the storm that remains. "Navigator to pilot. I will slowly count to three. On three, make your turn and start your descent." Slowly I start my counting: 1— 2—3.

Everyone begins looking for lights, either in the city or on the runways at the airport. I fold my maps; attach my parachute, and breath a prayer. "Lord, it's in your hands now. Please help us to land safely, if it is your will." It seems that we fly for an eternity in clouds and snow. There is nothing but blackness. The wind is relentless. The plane is bouncing in all directions. I expect any minute to hear the pilot say, "We're going up in preparation for bailing out."

"I see a light," shouts the bombardier, "Way over to the right." "I believe it is a runway," yells the copilot. The pilot is already fighting the plane to try to get it over to the runway before the runway ends. We hit the runway with a bang. The pilot and copilot use every emergency procedure they know to stop the plane. We stop less than ten feet from the end of the runway.

The airport official who meets our plane is amazed, "I don't know how you found a runway in this terrible storm. It is a miracle." The airport is closed, and we are hungry and need a place to sleep. We are not supposed to leave the airfield in our flying clothes, but an airport official says we have to leave. He loads us in the back of a truck and heads for the city. He locates a hotel with vacant rooms, and while our rooms are being prepared we rush to the tavern-grill in the hotel. We are starved.

The tavern is full of people. They hug us, pat us on the back, and shake our hands. "We heard your plane and expected to read in the morning that you had crashed."

"How do you want your steak?" yells the waiter. We reply that we need a menu to check the price.

"Don't worry about that. All food and drinks for you are on the house. Our customers are demanding the privilege of paying the bill."

Man, oh man! What a steak I have in front of me. It is the thickest steak I have ever seen in my life, and the waiter says we were eating "prime corn fed Iowa beef." The free drinks are being consumed rapidly, and by the time we finish the big steaks and have a delicious dessert, some are feeling great. The pilot stands up and proposes a toast. "I have heard many complaints recently about the caliber of the flight officers coming from mass production these days. But, this crew is very lucky. Crew 116 has the best flight officers in this Air Force. Tonight I propose a toast to our copilot and navigator. They may have saved our lives tonight. Here's to our copilot and navigator." The glasses clink, and the crew yells. The crowd in the tavern joins in the chorus.

The copilot proposes his toast. "You probably don't know what a tremendous job our pilot did in landing our plane in that horrible storm. Here's to the best B-17 pilot in Sioux City, Iowa." Again the glasses clink, and the crew yells.
Not to be outdone, I purpose my toast. "Here's to the best B-17 crew in all the world." I hold up my glass of coke and again the glasses clink. All is well with Crew 116.

Yes, Crew 116 is an excellent B-17 crew. All are well trained, and we operate as a unit. We have quickly built a "cocky" attitude, which will be necessary in combat. We think and act as if we are the best crew on base. We have finished our training and are ready for our orders, but they do not arrive. What is the difficulty?

The night of May 8 I hear shouting all over the camp. The war in Europe has ended. All in camp are excited. They will not have to fight immediately. I am a little disappointed. I am aware that many have been praying that I would not be sent to combat in Europe. I am not one of them. I want to complete my tour of duty as soon as possible so I can start living a normal life. Yes, if such is possible, I want to give love a try with Polly. I have had no opportunity for four years, seeing her only a few times each year and one year not seeing her at all and knowing all the time that Tom is number one in her heart.

I know that Polly is praying that I will not be sent into combat. I know she is a much stronger Christian than I. I guess her prayers get through and mine do not. There is no way I can be upset with her as long as she keeps the letters coming.

Polly is doing her practice teaching for a teacher's certificate. When she returns to the dorm, her friends begin hailing her with "Congratulations!" It was announced in chapel that she is the valedictorian of the graduating class. Martha reported that when her name was called, there was a tremendous response. As usual, she is modest, saying that all she will get out of this is the worry of making the farewell address for the class. I know she is just as pleased as I am. She is some gal.

There are thirteen more days of school at Campbellsville, with something special happening just about every night along with final tests. At the end of the letter, three short paragraphs please me very much.

> "I'd like at least one more letter from you while I am at Campbellsville."

"You'll get this, Polly, and a bit more. I have a surprise for you." She continues:

> I wish you'd be home soon, but I'm almost selfish enough to wish you wouldn't because I can't imagine your being there without my being over next door to pester. I think every time you have been home, I've been there at least for a tiny while. It's the separation from the Baskins that hurts most since we've moved. No kidding.

I love this paragraph. Polly has forgotten she could not get home when I stopped there on the way to Lincoln, Nebraska. I'm glad she could not get to Rocky Hill that time; otherwise I would have missed that wonderful second trip to Campbellsville.

Buddy, I'd like to tell you again how proud I am of you. I think I once, a long time ago, wrote something about your deserving a pat on the back. If you deserved it then, you deserve it much more now. I don't like to think of your being dissatisfied about staying in the States, but I do understand how you feel as much as an outsider could. Everything is going to be all right though.

Sioux City, Iowa, May 17, 1945. Polly, I want you to know my life isn't dull all of the time. Crew 116 really had a laugh when their navigator, namely me, had a little accident last Wednesday. You see, I was rushing through the bomb bay of the airplane when I accidentally caught the seat of my pants on a sharp piece of aluminum sticking out from the bomb bay frame. Well, you can imagine the rest. When we landed, four of my crew had to walk close behind me all the way to the barracks. Our enlisted men really enjoyed the incident, but, honest, I did not see anything funny about the "hole" affair.

I want you to know this. I don't know whether or not you will ever like me other than as a good friend, but I'm not worrying about it any more. I have placed the whole matter in God's hands. My prayer is that He will help me to say and do what is best for our relationship. The rest is up to you.

Giving thanks every day, not only for what you are, but for what you mean to me.

Your fly-guy

Polly writes it is 11:15 P.M., and she has a final test tomorrow, but she wants to write me before going to bed. She empathizes with my army temptations and shares with me some of the problems she will face after graduation. She says, "It isn't easy for me to talk about things like this, but I feel the need to share these thoughts with you tonight." I respond, "You had better quit saying things like that or you will have me going A.W.O.L. again. I do love that gal." Then she writes:

> "I too have put everything about my future in God's hands. Strange, how much easier things seem and how much happier one can be, isn't it? In my last letter I said I would like at least one more letter from you at Campbellsville. Well that one yesterday did not count. Crooked, ain't I?" Hebrews 12:1,2

> **Note sent with my picture, May, 1945.** I want to send this as a token of my appreciation for one of your many accomplishments. There are so many I am having a difficult time selecting the right one. Well, finally, I have selected one. Which one? Well, none of them in particular, but all of them in general. Congratulations, and thanks a million for being just what you are and meaning so much to me.

Whew! I'm really flying high – three letters from Polly in two weeks. I like it when she "graduates" if that is the cause of this attention. The last paragraph of her last letter says everything.

> Oh rats! That's not what I am wanting to tell you. But what I'm wanting to say I can't say so maybe it's just as well. The picture is – well, anyhow it means a lot to me. It's so like you that I'm using it for an audience to practice my speech. Hope it isn't too boring. I still haven't expressed

what I want to but—anyhow, you should have known better than to send the picture during exam week when you know I need to concentrate on books, not looks.

Ardmore, Oklahoma, June 25, 1945. I suppose you have already noticed from the letter heading that I am now at a new station. Really, the only way I can tell so far is the heat and the headache I have from spending two nights on a troop train.

One of our first missions was to fly to Abilene, Kansas to be a part of an air salute to General Ike for his homecoming, Friday. Well, all day Thursday we practiced for this mission. The hardest part of the whole deal was that we had to make a ninety-degree turn, which is very difficult in a thirty-six-plane formation. After the turn we were to fly directly up Third Street where people were massed on the street for a parade. It really was going to be a beautiful formation. As the planes got over the general's platform, they were supposed to dip the left wing. Just think, dipping a wing to a general. Thrill, thrill.

Just before we were ready to take off Friday, a storm appeared from nowhere, and we had to stay on the ground. I started back to the line from my plane when a bolt of lightning struck about one hundred yards away. At that time I was wading in about one half inch of water. Yip! If you think a frog can jump high for his size, you should have seen me. I think I broke the world's speed record getting into a building. I hate to admit it, but I was plenty scared.

Ardmore is a pretty dull place. There is a bit of excitement occasionally. Yesterday, a plane caught fire and burned in the air. You can't imagine the emotion involved in watching the crew bail out and counting 1 - 2 - 3 - 4 until each chute opened. I understand more and more each day why a certain general said there are no unbelievers in the air corps. I guess there was not a single person on the ground who was not uttering some sort of a prayer as guys tumbled from the plane. They all landed safely. Thank goodness!

Just when you think nothing is going to happen to you in the army, you get a big surprise. One morning I am told to start packing my clothes. I am being pulled from my crew, and will soon be on my way to Biggs Field, Texas to become the navigator of a B-29. Why me? It seems that they are planning some B-29 missions that will be navigator-oriented. From my record they think I meet their requirements. Little do they know that for the past few months I have become a sloppy navigator with no celestial practice.

Anyway, I am traveling by myself and have six days to get to El Paso, Texas. Of course, my first thought is, "Can I make it to Kentucky?" I am certain I am breaking all records for checking out of the Ardmore base, and I do manage to catch the next train and head for Kentucky. I know Kentucky is not on the route from Ardmore, Oklahoma to El Paso, Texas, but I am determined to see Polly, even if only for a few hours.

I make it to Rocky Hill, spent a few hours with my folks, borrow Dad's car, and am on my way to Bowling Green. Polly and her mother are cleaning the house. She is wearing what she calls her old worn out dress, which she wears only at cleaning times. She claims her hair is dirty and a mess. To me, she is beautiful.

The first afternoon we take a car ride into the country. Just touching Polly, holding her hand, thrills me beyond description. That night we sit in the living room and talk about the many happy times we have had together. Polly asks, "Remember a little girl's excitement at Christmas over a box of handkerchiefs from Kayo? I knew the gift was from you. I was just twelve and you were fourteen at that time?"

"Remember when I kissed your hand while we were practicing for a senior play?"

"That seems so long ago. I was so jealous when you would sit with Marge on the school bus. I could not understand why. Remember selling me one and one-half yards of pink-checked print when your folks were out of the store? Were you flirting with me?"

"What about the time the band boys' kite disappeared and two girls were accused of helping it disappear?"

"Remember the night you, Ned, and I walked home with Frances from a party and on the way back rang Brother Pierces' door-bell and ran?"

"One time your dad was sick, and I volunteered to split enough wood to last several days. You hid the chopping block, and I chased the wood all over the back yard."

"Remember typing some home economics notes for me once when you were home from Nashville? You asked me what on earth was meant by 'pinking material.' And remember when a gang of us got ukuleles, fiddles, sax, etc. and paraded up the road? You wore my red jacket, and I wore your high school athletic sweater."

"Remember when you dropped tobacco plants for two setters? I was one of the setters and really enjoyed working with you."

"Wasn't it terrible? I was so muddy. Remember when you came to Campbellsville. You really charmed all of my girl-friends."

"Too bad, I couldn't charm you the same way."

"Maybe you did."

"I wish it were true. You know I love you, Polly."

"That's because you don't really know me."

"If I don't know you now, I never will. Some day you are going to love me."

With a grin she replies, "You think so?"

The next afternoon we hold hands as we hike across the Western Kentucky University campus, admiring the beautiful flowers. The third night we enjoy popcorn as we look out Polly's kitchen window at the most beautiful moon I have ever seen. I accuse Polly of burning my hand while we are popping the corn. She makes like she is kissing it to make it heal. How I yearn for a real kiss that will cure my heart.

If heaven is anything like the three times I am with Polly on this short leave, then I am ready to go right now. There's nothing like being with the one you love. My heart is beating so fast for three days that I must have used up ten years of my life span. Polly loves me; I can tell. Maybe not nearly as much as I love her, but she loves me. I don't know why she won't express her feelings for me. She knows now I love her very much. I would pour out my love for her in so many ways, if she would just express in some way her feelings for me.

I debate what I will say in my next letter to Polly. I really want to send a scaled down version of the letter I am going to write when I leave the States for combat, simply telling her of the profound love I have for her. But maybe I should not do this. I ask about Tom, and she immediately changes the subject. She has no intention of letting me know anything about her relationship with Tom. I have to be very careful. I cannot lose Polly now. It would kill me.

The safe procedure I follow in this first letter is a mistake. Polly expects a much different letter because there is no question that I show my love for her in everything we do while I

am at home. Actually, Polly is a bit angry at me. This is great!
I am glad she wants me to express my love for her. I take this
to mean she has some feelings for me.

Biggs Field, Texas, July 27, 1945. Well tonight I am
out in the desert where the coyotes howl, and Maggie (a
star Polly had named) shines the brightest, and where the
moon beams nearly as bright as it does through a certain
willow tree in your back yard.

I want to emphasize again how much I enjoyed the
happy times with you on this furlough. I don't suppose I
will ever forget the many little things we did together, that
seemed to mean so much to me. (Okay, go ahead and call
me a sentimental old fool, but please leave out the old.)

When I arrived back in camp and tasted a cup of G.I.
coffee, I realized that I was not living in the perfect world
I was in the previous week. At this time I called on my
feeble brain to do a little thinking and finally reached the
conclusion that it definitely was not appropriate for me to
make some of the statements I made while at home. I have
introduced this subject before, but we never seem to discuss it. However, today, after drinking that potent cup of
java, I can clearly see that everything in this world cannot
taste good so I am willing to face the truth. Here are two
of the many arguments I can give on this subject.

Argument #1. It is true that you have a steady boy
friend, although so far I have refused to let myself think of
such a thing. I guess it is easier to live in a dream world
than to face reality..

Argument #2. What surprises me more than anything
else is that I say and continue to say things that should be
discussed jointly and not singularly. It is quite possible
that this will never be a reality. As I have said before, it is
much more pleasant to dream than to face the truth. I

have not one good reason to dream the way I do about your feelings for me in response to my sincere love for you.

Even if my actions were mistakes and my statements to you were not appropriate (the truth of which I am unable to convince myself), I am not the least bit sorry for anything I said or did because I enjoyed every moment with you. How can a person call happiness a mistake? From the bottom of my heart, I love you.

Buddy

Risking All For Love

The B-29 is a beautiful plane, streamlined and fast. Often in flying in the United States, the B-29 will fly past older fighter planes. This makes the pilots of the fighter planes very unhappy, especially when the crewmembers of the B-29 wave good- bye. The nicest thing about the B-29 is that it is pressurized and heated. We do not have to wear bulky clothes and oxygen masks. The B-29 is not designed for the navigator. To take celestial shots, the navigator has to crawl through a tube over the bomb bay to a bubble above the tube. There he searches for stars, takes his shots, and crawls back through the tube to a little worktable behind the pilot and co-pilot.

By the time I get to Biggs Field my crew is already formed, waiting for a navigator. A big redheaded Texan is the pilot of the plane. He is a bit older than the usual pilot, having flown planes for oil companies in Texas. Immediately I like his leadership ability.

Our mission is explained to us at our first briefing. As soon as we are trained, we will fly our specially equipped planes from the United States to the combat area. Our mission will be to fly across Japan and drop mines in the waters beyond Japan in order to disrupt commerce and weapons shipments. This means we will face anti-aircraft fire and fighter planes going and coming. We are told that the chances are great that many of our planes will be crippled and cannot stay with the formation. Each plane must be self-sufficient, able to fight off the enemy, and able to find the way home. The B-29s we will be flying are called stripped-ships. The radar unit and part of the bomb bay will be replaced by extra fuel tanks to allow for flying for longer periods of time.

Well, it seems I am on my way to combat again. In just a few weeks, we will fly to some airfield in the Pacific and be in combat immediately. However, there is one big change in my life. I have no concern now about the letter I will write to Polly before leaving for combat. She already knows that I love her very, very much.

Polly's letter in response to my short note, which I mail soon after my arrival at Biggs Field, indicates she is not one hundred percent perfect. She does have a temper. She does not want "thanks" for our wonderful times together during my leave. She wants a continuation of the expression of my love for her.

I write my second letter before I receive a letter from her, and she is not overly pleased with this letter either. She evidently wants me to love her without any doubts or questions concerning her feelings for me. I am willing to love her under these circumstances, but I feel I should at least point out some difficulties in our relationship. In spite of these problems, I indicate anew my sincere love for her. She does write enough to let me know I am an integral part of her life now, not just a good next-door neighbor- friend. She starts her letter with:

> Do you realize that you and you alone have the power to make me miserable or on the other hand, happy – a kind of happiness I'd never dared think of in connection with myself? I see right now that I must not finish this letter tonight. So, good-night.
>
> **Next morning**. I thought the daylight would make me more sensible, but I find that I still mean the last paragraph I wrote last night. It's the first time I have admitted it, and goodness knows I've fought against it and tried to laugh the idea away with everything that's in me. In spite of my efforts however, it remains a fact.

"Polly, Polly, Polly," I say to myself. "I believe you are beginning to love me. At least, I hope and pray that this is true. Why won't you just say that you love me instead of hinting at your love?" However, I am overjoyed with Polly's letter. My heart is beating much too fast.

Her next statement seems to be an answer to a question in my last letter.

> Last October I spent a week of utter hell – and I mean just that – trying to make an important decision in the direction that I knew in my heart was not in God's plan for me. Well, needless to say God won, for which I shall never cease being thankful, and the wonderful thing was that I found that God's way about the matter was really what I had wanted. I had merely been fighting it for fear of hurting somebody. I'd like to tell you about it, and maybe someday I will.

She certainly leaves a lot to my imagination. It could have been that Tom wanted to get married before going overseas, and she asked to postpone the marriage until he returned. It could have been that he wanted to get engaged so she would not date other boys while he was gone. It could have been she had a break-up with a boyfriend in Campbellsville.

What Polly told me is not enough to give me much confidence. I know of flowers and gifts she has recently received from Tom even though he is stationed in Europe. He is still an integral part of her life. I do not know of her relationships with boys at Campbellsville. All I know to do is to continue to build the foundation for the letter I will write before combat and depend on God for the rest.

Biggs Field, August 6, 1945. Did you ever hear of a guy going to chow, sitting through a whole meal and eating only two bites; or going to class and in the middle of the class the instructor reminds him that he is still wearing his hat; or sitting through six hours of important lectures without taking a single note; or walking to and from class with his crew and not saying anything so the crew thinks he is sick? Well this is what happened to me today. I guess this is the reason I am writing this letter now even though it is very late, and my crew flies tomorrow. But I know I will not be able to sleep until I share my thoughts with you.

I don't know whether you have ever experienced a time when everything seemed to go wrong. As we prepared for take-off a few days ago, we were the second plane in line on a runway. As the first plane moved down the runway, it was obvious that it would not be airborne before the end of the runway. The plane plowed into the desert sand, and the huge gasoline tanks exploded. Of course, all were killed instantly. The tower had not been notified that with our extra load of gasoline our planes could take off only on one long runway. I thought, "We could have been first in line."

Then another day, our plane had to land with two engines on fire. The little red truck rushed out to meet us, but all got out of the plane unharmed. These things upset a guy when he is already lonesome and blue because he has received no correspondence recently from the one he loves.

Please don't misunderstand what I am saying. I really am not the least bit scared – just a bit nervous. I don't know of anything I am scared of except you. Don't laugh at this statement because it is the truth. I have known for a long time that I liked you better than any girl I have ever known. It has been obvious to me that I have little control over my emotions as far as you are concerned. Before I left for my leave, I made specific plans to have a great time but not to do or say anything foolish. My plans did not work. To put it in plain words, I guess I've got it bad. I love you too much.

Because of your letter, I am a new person tonight. See what ten little words in your letter did to me. When I got to your words "You have the power to make me miserable or happy," I stopped reading. I know now that you feel a little of that which has "knocked me for a loop." My love for you is growing so rapidly that I'm not the same person any more. I pray that soon you will feel the same way. I refuse tonight to read the second page of your letter. I am afraid you will say something that will contradict the first page. I'll read the rest of it tomorrow. Even though it is late, I am tired, and I must get up early in the morning, tonight I am the happiest person in the world.

Biggs Field, August 8, 1945. I know it is not my time to write, but I seem to have lost some of my stubbornness, and if you can cause me to cease being selfish, I might turn into a fairly decent person after all. Who knows? I finally got enough courage to read the rest of your letter. Although I feel that you misunderstood my last letter, I think I understand your concern. I am sorry for the letter I wrote and for asking specific questions. I really should not have written that letter, but you can't imagine how miserable I was when I wrote it. Now, maybe you can see why you made me so happy by letting me know I have a chance to mean more to you than just a good friend.

Every second I was with you in Bowling Green was wonderful. There is just no way to describe it. You can't imagine how much I long to be with you again. Well, twinkle, this is a funny world, and I guess I am the funniest guy in it, but there is one thing about which I am certain, "I'm in love with you."

All preliminary flights for our B-29 training have been completed. It is now time to begin long distance flights, for the crew to discover whether they have a good navigator or a sorry navigator. This is important for their safety in the mission assigned to our B-29 crew. We are on our way to the west coast. I am told to relax and enjoy myself during the first part of the flight because I will be under severe pressure the last half of the flight. I move to a window to enjoy my first view of the west coast. We are flying below the clouds, and the view is breath-taking as we fly up the coast from Los Angeles to San Francisco. Soon after flying over San Francisco, I am told to take a thirty-minute nap. That is, I am not supposed to look out a window or to record any data from the instrument panel. My assignment is to get us back to El Paso purely by celestial navigation. It is easy to tell that we are gaining altitude, trying to get above the clouds.

Then I receive my orders. "The flight is yours. Direct us back to El Paso. We will maintain the same airspeed and direction until you give us your instructions." I immediately record all data from the instrument panel, and race through the tube to the bubble. Am I in for a shock! Most of the sky is covered with an extremely high overcast. I can see only a few stars in one small section of the horizon. I quickly take my shots, rush back to the table and draw the triangle. It is terrible! It is just what I expected, long and slim. We are somewhere within the triangle. But where? I guess that my estimation could be off by as much as 60 miles. This definitely is not a good start on my first crucial mission.

For the next few hours the sky is covered with thin clouds. At last there is a hole in the overcast, and I am able to get another set of shots. Again the only stars I can find are in one small section of the sky, and the triangle is lopsided. It seems that our path is off course from what I had projected. This is definitely not my lucky night. There is no break in the overcast before I have to give my final directions for El Paso and my estimated time of arrival. At the estimated time of arrival, I note we have to make a sharp turn to get to the field. I do not know how much we missed the field, because the pilot is trying to find the best way to get through the clouds. However, some of the crewmembers are not overly friendly. I know they are disappointed in their navigator. I am certain my results are good enough to meet specifications. At all fields in the Pacific there are strong radio signals. If one can get reasonably close to an island, you can easily locate the island. Anyway, that does not matter. What does matter is the opinion of my crew. The crew is not certain that they have a strong navigator.

The next flight is even more difficult for the navigator. During the first half of the flight I am to record all airspeeds and directions, and using recorded wind data, I am to keep a running plot of where the plane is located at all times. According to my calculations, we are flying over Florida. Then we make a simulated run of dropping mines in the Atlantic somewhere east of Jacksonville, Florida. The pilot immediately turns and starts gaining altitude. From my approximate computations, I give him a direction to get to El Paso and begin to direct him by celestial navigation the rest of the way. I rush to the bubble and see a beautiful sight. There are no clouds above us, and I can select my favorite stars. I take my shots and have a near-perfect equilateral triangle. I locate our plane in the middle of the triangle. Thirty minutes later I take three more shots in a clear sky. Ordinarily, I would have waited a bit longer for my second set of shots, but because of the experience in my last flight, I fear overcast might appear. I call in my corrections, double check everything, and do wait longer before taking the third set of shots. The sky is still beautiful, and my triangle is again perfectly equilateral. I check my true position with my projected position and am pleasantly pleased with the accuracy. We are rapidly approaching the Mississippi-Louisiana line.

The pilot calls and requests that in five minutes I give him a new direction and estimated time of arrival in El Paso. Thank goodness for my confidence because I am in for a big surprise: "Today we are simulating you have been wounded by flak. You will be unable to do any more navigating. Your last instructions are supposed to be good enough to get us close to home. Your work is over for the day. You can lie down and take a nap if you wish."

I have been working constantly for nearly nine hours. Believe it or not I do go to sleep. I have a good nap. I do not know what is going on until I hear one of the crewmembers say loudly, "I don't believe it." I get up and look out a window, and we are passing over the middle of a city. I check my watch to get an idea of what city. The watch says we should be directly over El Paso. Surely not – I cannot be that lucky. Wind velocity and direction and many other things change in the distance we have traveled since I gave my last instructions. Navigation is simply not an exact science.

The crewmembers joke and give me a hard time as we are getting out of the plane. They claim I have been shot and the engineer has to bring us home. "The engineer is a better navigator than the navigator." I know they are pleased with their navigator. We are going to be a great crew, full of confidence in each other.

The next day they are still teasing. I can tell they have bragged to the other crews about the accomplishments of their navigator. "He split the middle of El Paso with directions given some place in Mississippi." I feel good. Later a thought enters my mind. I guess I will never know whether I really had a fantastically lucky day or whether our commander checked my directions with the radio station in El Paso and was completely satisfied. Then occasionally along the way he made changes so small that the crew does not notice. He may have headed directly for the radio station in El Paso. He is a smart cookie, and this could have been his way of building the morale of his crew. I guess I'll never know.

✧

I live for my letters from Polly. Each letter assures me a bit more that Polly loves me. I can read one of her letters and be on a high for many hours. There is just one thing missing. Why won't she say, "I love you"? I read her next letter many, many times. I am certain she is saying indirectly that she loves me. It would have been so easy for her to close the letter with "Love, Polly."

No, I haven't answered your letter as soon as I might have, but I'm answering it as soon as I dared. I had to be sure what I'm going to write was what should be written, and not merely what I felt during an avalanche of emotion. It's been a day and a half since I received your letter. Now I'm certain of what I want to write although I may not be able to put it in words.

I can't tell you how many times I've read your last letter. I'm not attempting to analyze what all this means because its so wonderful and unbelievable. I cannot help but think of the first message by telegraph in connection with all of this, "What hath God wrought?" For certainly whatever it is, whatever it means, whatever the results may be – it is a work of God. It has been since you wrote back in the spring that you'd decided to let God take the reins, and since I gave up the miserable struggle I was making to manage things myself and found the peace of letting God manage my affairs—even those involving matters of the heart – it has been only since then that events have taken the path they're in now.

So evidently, Buddy, if things have been planned thus far, the outcome of it all is planned too. There are a lot of things that have to be figured out, but I feel confident that everything is in capable hands. I feel that with my hand in yours for renewed courage and God leading us both, everything is bound to work out satisfactorily.

Biggs Field, August 13, 1945. There is no need to say that I am a sentimental fool as you already know it, but I have read your last letter more than ten times already. In fact, it is just about worn out now. Each time I read it I want to take you in my arms and give you a big hug.

Guess whom I got a letter from today – Murl. I got quite a kick out of one part of his letter. It all started with a letter he wrote telling about a great date he had had. Not to be outdone, I wrote him that I had had a great time with a wonderful girl who now lives in Bowling Green. He seems to think that I am treading on someone else's territory. Maybe so! Maybe no! I don't particularly care. Guess I'm just made that way. Selfish? Huh? (I acted as if I did not care, but the fact that Polly would not say she loved me, and I did not know her relationship with Tom kept me awake many nights.)

Continue to pray for me that I may say and do the right things as far as you are concerned, for circumstances have now gone far beyond my power to be reasonable.

There is shouting all over the camp, and the Mexican firecrackers are going strong in El Paso. The war is over. Japan has surrendered and just in time. I like to think that this is the result of Polly's prayers. In just a few days I would probably have been flying across the Pacific. I was disappointed when I missed combat duty in Europe, but just the opposite is true now. I want nothing more than to get home to Polly. I do not know how long it will be until I receive my discharge. One day there is a rumor that we will be a part of occupational duty, and the next day the rumor is that we can get out in a hurry if we will join the army air force reserve. Indeed, the war is over. But can we make this world a better place to live? Polly summarizes our problems in her next letter.

> My heart is so full of everything that all I can say is, "Thanks be unto God for His wonderful power." I found myself immediately thinking – this means Buddy will soon have a chance to fulfill whatever service he has to give the world.
>
> We were awakened this morning, August 14, at 1:00 A.M. by all the sirens, fire alarms, etc. after the first report was given of the surrender. Of course, it was unofficial until tonight. We got up at once and dressed and went downtown. I hate to be pessimistic, but I believe you will understand my next statement. It makes me fearful for our posterity, the next generation, to see the way we are celebrating this "longed for" day. I strained my ears to hear someone giving credit to whom credit is due, our Lord. But instead, drunken hilarity and profanity fell harshly on my ears.

My next letter to Polly is written in what she calls her last week of liberty. Yes, she will become a schoolteacher next week. She approaches this time with some anxiety.

> Hello schoolteacher! I bet you are having a good time this week as you begin your work as a teacher. You will be great, just like you have been in everything else you have done. God has given me assurance that everything will be easy for you.
>
> We are just about through our training on B-29's. To-day was a fairly good day except I had to work very hard. We were in the air until about 6:00 P.M., and by the time we had stored our equipment and serviced the plane for

the next crew, it was about sundown. I rushed to the mess hall because I was very hungry. On the way back to the BOQ from the mess hall, I saw the most beautiful moon I've seen since we looked through the morning glory vine in your back yard. Anyway, I just could not go to bed without having a little chat with you. Right now in my dreams I am squeezing your hand and looking into a pair of twinkling eyes.

The latest rumor is that we will be sent overseas as a photo recognizance group. In other words we will be assigned the job of taking pictures of all Japan and part of China to enable the United States to have accurate maps of the area. There will probably be a different rumor next week. It is certainly hard on a person to have happiness staring him in the face and then be drawn back behind a curtain into darkness. Anyway, I know there is a God that can hold our hands together even though we are thousands of miles apart if He thinks it is best.

Biggs Field, August 29, 1945. I really have a good one to tell on myself. If you remember while I was at home I mentioned the fact that nylon hose could be purchased in Mexico. Well, the other day I decided to go shopping in Mexico. I bought an alarm clock so now I can get up on time. While I was shopping I noticed quite a lot of hose on display so I searched until I found a nice looking gray haired lady who looked very trust-worthy, and inquired about nylon hose. From her I purchased a package of hose which (to quote the lady) were the best nylon in Mexico, would wear like pre-war nylon, and were the last ones in the store.

When I got back to the BOQ that night I decided to gloat over the results of my purchasing ability when I happened to notice in small print that my purchase was not nylon but cotton. The fact is I now have hose on my hands. Since the air corps forbids its officers from participating in the better things of life such as wearing fancy hose, I am mailing them to you even though they are not nylon. Please do not wear them in public as I no longer believe the "dear old lady" who guaranteed them not to rip, ravel, tear, or run down to the heel.

However, Twinkle, I want to inform you that in the box you will receive is something very valuable to me so do not throw it away with the hose. In the box is a little trinket presented to a certain person on January 4 of this year. There were two of these trinkets presented to him – you know the old tradition—one for the mother and one for the girl you love. Is there any more a guy can say?

To me, Twinkle, the conquering of hard problems seems to make life more wonderful. Happiness is the ability with God's help to ride over the heavy waves of hardships and reach land safely. As a teacher, one may fail in trying to make a child understand that $2 + 2 = 4$, but think of the satisfaction of learning that she is very good in reciting poems or drawing pictures. At the end of every struggle, of every day's work there is a reward if you will only look for it. This is what makes life so wonderful.

The thing that makes a person enjoy life is work. I don't mean work, as most people know it "to buy pleasures that last for such a short time." I mean the continual fight to obtain a higher level physically, mentally, and spiritually. Planning for the future, working to obtain the highest levels, helping each other attain these levels, the sharing of success and failure – most of my married friends do not possess this happiness. I might add that I have never met but one girl in my life that made me want to reach these high levels. To her now I say, "I love you."

Polly's letters keep me from going crazy while waiting for army decisions. My letters must be helpful to her.

Your letters, written in any mood, mean more to me than I ever dreamed written words could mean. Ordinary letters are useless after one reading, but not yours. Sometimes I tell myself I'm completely daffy when I get to thinking of the effect a letter from you has on me. I know this sounds silly, but it would not if you ever got a wonderful letter like those you write to me. Nothing you could give me would mean as much as the wings. I'll do my best to be the girl who should wear them.

On Monday I learn we do not have a duty assignment for Tuesday, and might not have one for several days. I am so homesick for Polly that unreasonable thoughts enter my mind. Suppose I can get a three-day pass for Wednesday, Thursday, and Friday. A good tip to the right person might accomplish this goal. Then if I leave early Tuesday morning I might be able to see Polly Wednesday night. Yes, I would be AWOL Tuesday, but I have no duty assignment; yes, I would be AWOL Saturday and maybe part of Sunday, but again we are not having duty assignments on weekends. Who can think reasonably when they are in love?

There's no way to describe my time with Polly during these three days. My heart races just looking at her. When I touch her, I am scared it will jump from my body. I get to Bowling Green in time for prayer meeting Wednesday evening. I am holding her hand, looking directly at the preacher, but seeing in my mind my beautiful Polly.

As we are getting in the car after prayer meeting, I have to take time to look into Polly's bright eyes to see if the twinkle is still there. As I am feasting on her beauty, completely absorbed by being so close to her, it happens. That's right! Without warning, she kisses me! It isn't a long kiss or the kind you might see in the movies. But when our lips touch, I know this memory will last forever. I had determined I would kiss Polly only when she told me that she loved me, but that soft kiss on my sorely neglected lips just has to be answered. Right there in front of the First Baptist Church, she gets the kiss that has been secretly stored for her for many years. I am certain that this emotionally loaded kiss indicates to her beyond words what she means to me. At least it opens the door for me to show I love her more than words can describe.

If Wednesday night is wonderful, then Thursday night is heaven. At the end of a school day I am waiting for Polly at Oakland School, where she teaches, in Dad's car with plenty of gasoline and a picnic basket prepared at Dad's store. We know of a special picnic spot. Polly is wearing a red (my favorite color) gabardine dress (purchased for the next time I come home). Oh my, she is beautiful.

It is a warm September day, so we drive with the windows down with the wind blowing our hair in all directions. We do not care – it is so wonderful being together. I assure Polly I am a great left-handed driver. My right hand is assisting the wind. I enjoy "mussing up" her hair. The Lord provides a beautiful fall day. The food is good. I stop eating periodically, take her in my arms and give her a big kiss, letting her know there are plenty of kisses left after that first one. There is a bountiful supply just for her. Yes, being with Polly is just like being in heaven.

I go to Oakland School to get Polly Friday afternoon and take her to Rocky Hill to be with me during my last meal with my folks. She is with my family that evening as they take me to the train station. Of course I would rather have had these last hours alone with Polly. However, she does seem to appreciate my wanting her to be with my family. She is touched by my many indications of how much she means to me. I think my parents and my sister have known for some time what Polly means to me, but it is good for them to experience firsthand my feelings for her. They are very pleased because they love Polly nearly as much as they love me.

My three-day pass has expired. Will the M.P.'s ask to see my pass tomorrow or Sunday? Who knows? Even if I should get in some difficulty, I am glad I decided to take the chance. There is no question in my mind now that Polly loves me. For this assurance, I would risk my life, and I have only risked the possibility of being AWOL.

Longing To Hear "I Love You"

How lucky can you get? I arrive back in El Paso, Texas without difficulty. No one checked my pass after Friday evening. Since the war is over, soldiers have a great deal of freedom on weekends. I am glad I took the risk of being classified as AWOL, because my time with Polly was indescribable. Even if I had been cited by an M.P., I think all that would have happened to me would have been a reprimand. This might have kept me from getting a promotion, but who wants a promotion. All I want is OUT.

Riding a train by myself from Kentucky to El Paso affords opportunity for day dreaming and thinking. There is no question that I am madly in love with Polly. She is an integral part of my every thought and action. It has been many months since I have had any interest whatsoever in another girl. My whole future is being planned around Polly. I have one problem. Doubts continue to cloud my mind. Why?

Polly refuses to discuss with me her present relationship with Tom. I drop the subject immediately Thursday evening when she shows a reluctance to answer a simple question, "How is Tom?" I am glad I did not press the issue because it might have resulted in a quarrel. Instead, Thursday evening was perfect. Polly's actions and statements completely validate that she loves me. Yet, there still seems to be a problem. I do not see how she can have any doubts about my love for her. Could it be that she is still not certain of her love for me?

I discard at least ten plans of action before arriving in El Paso. After my July visit with Polly, I put pressure for some answers. This caused her to be angry at me for two weeks. I would like to request some answers in my next letter. No, I won't do this. I simply cannot do something that will cause her to be angry at me. My plan at this time is to try to do and say things that will lead her to know she loves me. Hearing "I love you" from Polly would completely erase all my doubts.

Biggs Field, September 27, 1945. This is Sunday night, two days since I last saw you. I arrived in El Paso about two hours ago, and found that no one seemed to miss me. There is no way to describe how great it was to be with you. Of course, Thursday night was perfect. Thanks be to God for such a wonderful leave and such a wonderful girl.

I forgot to tell you that I liked your school very much, and I think you have a very interesting group to teach. However, I disagree with you that you sometimes become discouraged and want to quit. I believe this is only your imagination playing tricks on you. My prayers are that the rest of the school year will be as happy and successful as the first five weeks.

You need to be careful when we are together because I love you so much that I take molehills and make mountains out of them. A good example of this was what you

said just before I left your house Thursday night. Better
set me straight because I love you so much now, I may not
be able to face the truth. No matter what happens, Polly,
please remember these three words, "I love you."

My next letter from Polly is as perfect as my trip home.
No, she does not say she loves me, but she calms my doubts.

I can't even think of a sensible way to begin your letter. My heart is so full that I can't be reasonable. This past
week has been so different to those preceding it that my
whole being has wanted to burst out in song. Sometimes I
get so happy that I think surely someone will ask me what
on earth is causing such loud hammering of my heart. In
spite of the fact that I miss you so much, in spite of the
fact that hope of an early discharge seems years away, in
spite of the fact that I catch myself approaching bitterness
because you have to be so far away, in spite of all this and
everything else discouraging, I am still basically so happy
– well, I just can't explain it.

Then she thrills my heart with her answer to my question
in the last letter.

The mountains you are afraid you are building out of
molehills have been mountains for ages. And as for what I
said as you left Thursday night listen closely because I'm
going to set you straight on this matter. Please believe me
it was not said on impulse. The meaning of the statement
and all else it signifies has been a fact in my mind since a
night in July when you and I were popping popcorn. Before that I wondered if I was imagining things. After that
night I knew my own heart.
      After I had gone to bed, Mom came in my room for
something and found me lying there half asleep with the
old khaki sock full of holes clutched in my hand. (You

know the one you sent me as a joke saying it needed mending.) Has she teased me! But I don't care. There's no need for my trying to keep anything from her because she knows me too well. Besides, I haven't tried to keep her from knowing. To be honest, I think she knew where my heart was long before I fully realized it myself.

Biggs Field, Early October, 1945. Want to know something! I love you! Surprised! Nope! Do you know when you mean the most to me? I don't really appreciate the pureness and fullness of my love for you until I stop to thank God for His many blessings on my life; then I realize how unworthy I am of the love I have for you. Even if we live to be a thousand years old, you will never be able to realize just what you mean to me. Sure, I love my father and mother. I love my sister more than any brother I know, but the affection and love I have for you is altogether different.

I don't know what is going to happen to me in the days ahead. There is still a possibility that I might be shipped overseas. But no matter what happens please remember this: With our faith in each other and with God as our guide, we'll be able to trudge through the dark night, and we know for certain there'll be a bright glorious day when the sun rises in the morning.

Finally Polly tells me that she loves me. I have known for some time that she loves me, but for some reason she would not write or say it. Here is part of my answer.

Guess what I did with your last letter. I cut three words from it and glued them on the back of your picture. I'm sure you know the three words I am talking about. They are the three words I have been longing to hear for a long time. Yes, in your last letter you wrote I love you. Thank you so much, darling. I have known for some time that you loved me. I just longed to hear or see it.

Just saying she loves me inaugurates a whole new era in my letters from Polly. She has such a wonderful way of describing how much I mean to her. Yes, she thrills my heart beyond all bounds.

It is interesting to note how I enjoy going places where we have been together: prayer meeting, church, school, and even home has a nearness to me because you have been there. The things we've laughed about have a double significance and are twice as funny now. Things we've talked about along a more serious line are doubly serious now. Friday I was standing at the front entrance of school staring in that glass door where we looked at our reflection that afternoon. Remember? The picture was the same – golden rod in the background, same girl, etc. – everything except you. I thought my mind was my own, but evidently Mom read my thoughts because she slipped up and whispered, "Stop your staring. You can't see what you saw when he was here."

Yes, Buddy, everything makes me think of us. Everything is so wonderful, so good, and yes so heavenly. Sometimes I get to thinking that something might happen to our love, but then I am okay again because we are both in God's hands. Buddy, Buddy, the wonder of it all comes up within me until it's just too much.

✧

Polly and Martha are going to meet at a student state convention to be held at Campbellsville College. I write a special letter to Polly as a surprise when she gets home. She writes me each of the three days she is at the convention. The first night she describes a devotional at a huge bon fire.

> At the close of the devotional, an opportunity was given for reconsecration and dedication. It was wonderful watching those fine Christian young people go quietly through the firelight.
>
> And Buddy, you were with me, holding my hands. I am sure that God does have a special purpose for everyone, certainly for you and me. I feel sure too that my special purpose is to be fulfilled through being with you, and that is as much as God is yet ready to reveal to me. I started to go forward and acknowledge that I had found my special place, but it seemed that God was telling me to wait until you and I could take that step together.
>
> Today I attended a conference on *Maximum Christianity in Building a Christian Home*. I wish you could have been with me, and whether you know it or not you really were here, holding my hand.

Biggs Field, October, 1945. For the past two weeks I have been worrying and praying over two important problems. I can't find the right answer myself so I am transferring these problems to you for a solution. Maybe together we can find the answer.

First of all, I am sick of having the wonderful joy of loving you locked up inside me. I want so much to let the world know how much you mean to me. The desire to tell the world how much I love you has haunted me day and night. I know the only way to accomplish this is to ask you to marry me, and if you are foolish enough to accept, then to announce our engagement. I have been postponing this for one reason. Everything so far has been – well, it has not been like the actions of most young people—and I so wanted to do this right. I was able to restrain myself a little by hoping for a furlough soon so I could ask you to marry me in the right way. Now it seems it will be at least thirty days before I get a furlough. I find I am unable to hold myself together any longer.

Polly, darling, what I want more than anything else in this world is to send you an engagement ring and tell the world how much I love you. Will you accept it?

Okay, while I'm being brave, I might as well get the other problem off my chest. I don't see any reason to wait until I finish college before we marry. Yes, I'm selfish in this matter, but I have prayed and prayed, and I still can't see any reason to wait that long. Maybe, I did not interpret correctly one of your letters in which you said not to let anything happen until I finished school. I got the indication that you thought we should wait that long.

Please do not misunderstand what I am writing. I'm not trying to rush you. In fact, I love you so much I would wait 5, 10, or 20 years, if necessary, but I don't see any reason. I am not trying to start an argument. I guess I just want you to remember this in your prayers, and we will have plenty of time to discuss it when I am home on furlough Christmas. Polly, I have said a lot in this letter, but I just had to say it. Please forgive me if I have done wrong.

Darling, regardless of the reply to this letter, just remember I'll still be loving you forever.

I Say Goodbye To Uncle Sam

On Monday morning Polly writes the shortest but most powerful letter I have received from her. Of course, I have slept very little since I mailed my last letter to her. I have known for several months that she loves me. Now, I am certain that she loves me with the same devotion that I have for her. I have no idea what the future holds for us. However, it is so much easier to face an unknown future with someone you love.

Monday Morning. Daddy is already in the car, and I've got to leave for school, but I just had to write a short note. Listen closely! With all the love God gave me to love a man, I love you. And it is God's will that it be that way. And now you know the answers to your questions. I will write a complete letter tonight.

Forever yours,
Polly

The letter I receive from Polly written that evening is precious. First she describes her reaction to my concern that our romance is not the typical story found in romantic novels.

There's no telling what I will say in this letter because my heart is playing a rollicking game of leapfrog with my lungs and ribs or something. First of all, Buddy, please do not say any more about the fact that our courtship has not been just "so and so." Who on earth wanted it that way? If everything had happened according to the usual run or things, it just wouldn't have been us. Perhaps everybody in love feels this way, and I grant them the right, but I still say *our love* is gloriously different. It has lived and thrived despite so many odds – despite the fact that a weaker flame would have smothered long ago for lack of air – despite the fact that God has led us into some pretty deep water before showing us the landing place.

Then she responds to my asking her to marry me. She knows how to thrill my heart. Polly, Polly, Polly, I love you so very much.

I had answered with God's assurance both of your questions long ago. So here goes the verdict. Hold tight, and if you want to jump out, it's too late now. Relative to the first question, I'm afraid I haven't thought as prudently as you. You say that the only way we can let the world know how much we love each other is to announce our engagement. Well darling, engagement or not, I've been dropping some pretty strong hints, and I keep hoping somebody will ask me point blank what I think of you so I can tell them with all my heart.

There is but one person in the world whose ring I shall wear. The ring will not make my love for him any greater because it's the man I love. However, I shall love the ring because of the giver and because of what it symbolizes. In other words, the answer is yes—my darling. My high school ring was 6 $\frac{1}{2}$, but please take heed. Will you please wait until you come home? In other words, I want you with the ring. So don't mail it.

Now here is the answer to the second question. Just you try waiting five, ten, or twenty years for me and see what I do to you young man. Five years from now I will be twenty-five, in ten years I will be thirty, and in twenty years I will be forty. No sir! Seriously, darling, when I wrote what I did about your not letting anything keep you from going on to college, I was attempting to be unselfish because I knew that you had something to give the world, and you made a statement about not going on to school if it meant putting off more important things. That made me think you'd let me stand in your way, and I could not bear the thought of that. Ruth 1:16-17

Biggs Field, late October, 1945. It is now five o'clock, and I have been trying to write you a letter ever since mail call this morning. See what effect you have on me. I have tried to write a letter for five hours and have written only three lines. Right now I am looking into those big eyes and talking to you as you smile at me from your high perch on my locker shelf.

I really should not write this letter now because I'm not physically qualified. You see my pulse rate is sixty to seventy beats a minute too fast, and my heart is jumping sideways. I expect any minute for it to come flying out across the room. In case you get this letter unfinished and all bloody, you will know that my heart flopped out on the table, and I had to quickly report to the hospital to get it repaired. My Bible states:

So men ought to love their wives as their own bodies. He that loveth his wife loveth himself. For this cause shall a man leave his father and mother and the two shall be one flesh. This is a great mystery.

Whatever this mystery is, it has happened to me. This is how much I love you, darling, and will continue to do so until the end of time. Concerning the ring, sweetheart, I'll gladly wait until I come home to give it to you. Since we are waiting until then, will you do me a favor? I don't know what is customary, and I don't particularly care so I suggest you and I select the ring together. I want to get a ring that you like as well as cherish for what it means. Just one more important thing! You've got to promise me you won't select a cheap ring. It has to be nice to go with our love.

Biggs Field is overflowing with soldiers. In fact, there are more soldiers than the field can handle. So there is a welcomed announcement. All flight crews on this base will get a thirty-day furlough, either in early November or in early December. I am overjoyed. Sometime soon I will place a lovely ring on the finger of my beautiful Polly. You can imagine how ecstatic I am when it is posted on the bulletin board that our crew will get a furlough in early November.

For three days I work very hard to get everything ready for an early start when the furlough papers are ready. I take my dirty clothes to the cleaners, and throw away all of my junk so I can clean my room. All day Wednesday I work clearing the field, which consists of turning in all flying equipment, paying all bills, and turning in my bedding.

At 5:00 P.M., Wednesday the orders are not ready. Finally, the announcement is made that they will be released at 5:00 P.M., Thursday. Wednesday night I sleep without pillows, without anything except my sweat suit and raincoat. All day Thursday I am excited and restless. I am one of the first people in line at 5:00 P.M.. I grab a set of furlough orders and rush back to the BOQ to get my bags and catch a taxi to the railroad station. I decide to inspect the list to make certain my name is spelled correctly. Wham! Bam! Am I in for a surprise! My name is not on the list. I run back to the orderly room and inquire about the mistake. From sergeant to lieutenant to captain to major I go, but no one knows anything. I say to myself, "Typical army." What can the trouble be? Finally I get the answer, "I guess the typist made a mistake and left your name off the list."

Telegram to Polly. Furlough Delayed. Will Write Tonight. Buddy

In my letter I explain to Polly what I know about the mistake. However, she cannot understand why they could not just type my name at the end of the list. It all sounds so reasonable, but the army does not function in a reasonable manner. The last two paragraphs in my letter to Polly describe my loneliness.

Tonight I sit, lonely and blue – no furlough, no letter, no nothing. When I look at my clothes all to be unpacked and put in place, when I look at my bed without sheets or blankets, and when I think of the thirty day wait until I can hold you in my arms, I admit I am very blue. But I am so grateful that no matter how terrible I feel, it never affects my wonderful love for you.

I love you, darling, and long more and more to be with you, but until that wonderful day arrives, I am trusting God to guide, direct, and keep us as He would have us to be.

I do not trust the army. The excuse they use for leaving my name off the furlough list is a bit of baloney. I have a good friend who works in the major's office; two months ago he secured for me a three day pass. This good friend promises to investigate, whenever he has the opportunity to be alone with records, if any other names are missing from the furlough list.

Polly's letters are wonderful. They keep me going through this period of my life.

Think of all the things we have to look forward to sharing together forever, just commonplace things such as listening to radio programs, watching the trees bud in the spring, devotional hours together, listening to rain against the window panes and on the roofs, looking forward to visits from your folks and mine. We'll be so proud of our home wherever it is. Oh, my goodness! I must not let myself get carried away like that, but it's all so wonderful. I just heard on the radio *My Buddy*. For me, this song has always meant you.

Night's are long since you went away
I think about you all through the day
My Buddy, My Buddy
No Buddy quite so true

Miss your voice, the touch of your hand
Just long to know that you understand
My Buddy, My Buddy
Your buddy misses you.

My good friend does take time to look at an old copy of the furlough list for November. Yes, someone has gone through this list and marked off a number of names. He recognizes some of the names that have been removed because they are to get furloughs just before they are sent to special assignments. There were a few names marked off that do not fit this category as far as he can determine. He does notice one thing about these names. These soldiers seem to have been in the army about a year longer than most of those on the November furlough list. I am in this category. He says he has no idea why my name was removed, but if he had to make a guess, he would guess that I would be getting a discharge before the rest of my crew. Thus it is natural to transfer me from my present crew.

I cannot give this information to Polly. She will believe I am among those selected for a special assignment. I determine I will be optimistic and believe I am among those who will get an early discharge. Could this occur at the time of my December furlough? Polly's letters keep my mind off what is going to happen to me.

> Buddy dear, I don't deserve all the things you think of me or plan for me. You must not think me better than I am. I'm not good, but I will say that I feel that I'm better since I've known of your love for me. It makes me want to be perfect for you and for God, but I fall so short. The ring idea is perfect. It will mean more because we select it together. Oh, darling, I do love you.

Biggs Field, Middle of November, 1945. Well, I guess I am just about the happiest man in the world right now. Boy, do I feel wonderful. Yes, I got a letter from you this morning. One of the guys commented, when he came by to get me to go to lunch with him and found me lying on my back with a "precious" letter in my hand and my eyes glued on the ceiling, "Well, Baskins got another letter from his girl. Who's going to do his work this afternoon?" Don't worry, honey, this is my lucky day and the major has not found a job for me yet.

All of a sudden, Polly becomes concerned about what her father might think about our engagement. This generates for me a thousand bad thoughts. Is she really concerned about her father, or is she asking for more time? She first said we would purchase a ring just as soon as I got home.

Polly, I'm not going to deny the fact I love you so very much I do not want to wait for anything. But if your father does not want you to wear my ring when I come home, we will wait a while. However, I simply do not believe this will happen. When he sees how much I love you and you love me, everything is going to be okay. The decision is yours. I love you very much, darling, and that is all that really counts. Everything will naturally work out for the best.

I have some great news. Should I tell Polly immediately, or should I share this news with her a little at a time? There's no way I can keep this good news from Polly.

Biggs Field, November 18, 1945. I don't know whether you will be able to read this letter as I am writing in a B-17 almost 10,000 feet above the ground, and I am trying to write on a flimsy book. I've been trying for several days to get my four hours in the air so I will get the extra flying pay, and it looks like I am going to make it today. Boy, is this plane loaded! There are six of us crammed in the nose section. You can imagine how many are in the rest of the plane.

Polly darling, I don't think I'm going to buy any civilian clothes until after Christmas. I think clothes will be cheaper in Bowling Green after that time. What am I saying? Did I let the cat out of the bag? Did I say that when I come home in December that it would be something besides a regular furlough?

When you get this letter it will be less than two weeks until I can hold you in my arms. Don't worry, honey. I'll love you just as much as a civilian as an officer in the air force.

Polly keeps me going with her wonderful letters.

I had planned to write this morning, and Mr. Smarty, it's all your fault that I didn't. I sat down at the dressing table to comb my hair in a hurry, so I'd have time to write. I combed and combed, and the more I combed, the more messed up it became. Suddenly, a suspicion began to grow. I shifted my eyes over to a picture of a certain guy with eyes that make you sort of double up inside, and sure enough there he was with such a mischievous twinkle in those eyes and an impish smile that I knew I'd caught the culprit. You rascal why do I love for you to mess up my hair? I love you and need you always.

In late November I write Polly a crazy letter. The last paragraph contains wonderful news.

Well, sugar-doll, I don't have much time for writing a letter. I have so much that I must accomplish in a short period of time. But I just could not wait another minute to tell you the good news. I just received word that I am going to leave Friday night for home. I should be in Bowling Green Sunday afternoon late (December 2). Darling, you'd better sleep all Sunday afternoon because I'm going to keep you up late Sunday night. Gee, but I love you.

The next day I receive a birthday card from Polly. That girl has a way of saying things that start my heart beating way too fast.

> Someday, maybe you'll know partly just what the day you were born means to me. Right now, this card will have to do, because I'm not buying a birthday present until I'm sure you're a civilian.
> So for now, have the most wonderful birthday ever, and my prayer is that we may be together for all your future birthdays, and that I may have the heaven-sent privilege to make them the happiest possible for you. Love forever.

There is no way to describe my reaction when Polly answers the door the first Sunday I am at home. She is so beautiful. She is wearing the red dress that is my favorite. This is the first time I have seen her since she said that she loved me, and the first time I have seen her since she said that one day she would be my wife. Even before I give her a kiss and take her in my arms, my heart is beating much too fast. She is mine, all mine, and I cannot believe it. Yes, I take time to breath a prayer, "Thank you, Lord."

During my first week at home, I am at Polly's house just about every afternoon when she gets home from school. She once described how much my letters meant when she arrived home, tired and worn out. I tease her that I might be a poor substitute, but she will have to be satisfied having me instead of the letters. Some evenings we dine at a local restaurant, but most of the time we eat the great meals cooked by her mother. Her mother can prepare the best meals in the shortest period of time of any person I have ever known. I surely hope some of this talent rubs off on Polly.

Well, it happens in spite of my efforts to prevent it. I am no longer a dashing air force officer but am rapidly becoming the serious-minded old country boy, Buddy Baskins. When with Polly I continue to wear my officer's uniform, as I am on Uncle Sam's payroll through January, 1946. In Rocky Hill, I wear old pre-army clothes.

After the first week at home, I am bored beyond description with nothing to do besides sit and rest. I am ready to go to work. Mom and Dad know I am planning to enter Western Kentucky University, but they suggest, "Why don't you work in the store until you start college?" Dad wants to get out of the store more often, and mother needs more time at the house to take care of her mother. So the second week at home I become a merchant. Most people think I have come home to take over the store. I do not tell them differently, and in a short period of time, I am an integral part of the merchandising business.

December and January are wonderful months. I am busy all of the time, working in the store all-day and looking into Polly's beautiful eyes three or four nights a week. I try to be with her Wednesday evenings for prayer meeting and Sunday evenings for Training Union and church. Mother and Dad use the truck on these two nights so I can have the car to go to Bowling Green. Also, I try to be with her on either Friday or Saturday evenings or both. These are our fun times. However, all of our times together were fun times to me; just being with Polly thrills me beyond all bounds. Some of our friends joke that they cannot be in Bowling Green without seeing us walking around the square holding hands.

We enjoy being together so much that we simply do not have any arguments. I worship this gal. There is just one small problem. Although we walk by the jewelry store, look at rings displayed in the window, and even look at rings in the showcase several times, Polly seems hesitant about selecting a ring. She fell in love with a dashing air force officer. Does she now love plain Buddy Baskins?

One Friday night while working in the store, I learn that Tom has just returned home with a discharge from the army. For some time I have suspected that the delay in our engagement has a great deal more to do with Tom than it does with Polly's father. I suspect that he wired flowers to Polly for Christmas. For the first time since Polly said she loved me in November, and we were to be engaged immediately, doubts begin to creep into my thinking. I immediately go to the bank and secure enough money to purchase a ring, more expensive than Polly will probably accept.

The next day, I am at Polly's house for my usual Sunday afternoon date. We then go to Training Union and church together. Then it is back to Polly's house for our Sunday night hours together before beginning a new workweek. To me these are the most enjoyable hours of the week, talking about our problems for the week, and sharing our suggested solutions to these problems. It is wonderful being in love. The times we are together Wednesday nights, Thursday nights, and Sunday nights are the stimuli that keep me going through the week.

On this Sunday night, I push Polly a bit more than usual for affection, and she responds admirably. Yes, she still loves me. I hate to interrupt such a wonderful evening, but before time to leave, I reach for my wallet and start removing twenty-dollar bills.

"What's that?" she asks.

"This is money for our engagement ring."

"But we have not decided upon a time."

"Didn't you say last November you were ready to wear my ring to let everyone know we are in love?" I ask, trying to be as loving as possible but also very firm.

"Yes."

"And we postponed getting the ring in order to find the ideal time to present the idea to your dad."

"Yes."

"I have been praying about this matter for more than three months. Let's talk to him now."

"Maybe I need to 'feel him out' a little at a time."

"Honey, I thought this was what you have been doing for the past three months."

It seems as if she is going to cry, and I love her too much to start an argument. I take both of her hands and look into her eyes as I have done so many times in the past few weeks. "Sweetheart, you know how much I love you, and you say you love me the same way. Don't you think your dad understands this by now?"

"I guess you are right, but I am not certain."

I want to say, "I think it is something else that is bothering you." Somehow I am able to control my tongue. "Well, I'd better go or your dad will be upset because it is getting late, and we don't want to give him an excuse to be upset. Do we?"

"But what about the money?" she asks.

"When I look at that stack of bills, I do not see money. I see a beautiful engagement ring, and it is yours. I'm giving it to you tonight. When you wear it is left up to you."

"But I can't keep that much money. What will I do with it?"

I glance around and see the large family Bible on a table in the living room. I open the Bible and spread the money between several pages in the middle of the Bible. "Your ring is stored in the Bible. How appropriate! God gave us our love for each other. Now He holds your ring."

Polly is not overly happy with me, but she does kiss me goodnight. It is a miracle that we get through this confrontation without a serious argument.

My heart is sad as I stumble from Polly's house. Hundreds of terrible thoughts are racing through my mind like ants on a sugar bowl. The fact that Polly continually refuses to discuss with me her relationship with Tom keeps sweeping through my mind. "Maybe she is still engaged to Tom. But I know Polly loves me. I also know she loves me very much. But is it possible for someone to be in love with two people? Could she be in love with both Tom and me? What a mess that would be! What if she cannot decide between us?"

Then there is a sad remembrance, "For more than five years Polly preferred Tom to me. Maybe she still does. I've done all I know to do. Everything is in Polly's hands, now. All I can do is pray for God's guidance."

The thoughts of Tom just holding hands with the one I love so very, very much is more than my mind can handle. What if he kisses her? I kick all four tires on the old ford, but nothing seems to calm my fears.

Polly's Influence On My Life

It's difficult to believe, but evidently it is true. Most of the letters, notes, and mementos in the two cigar boxes have been removed. Yet, Polly's influence on my life seems just as strong as ever. How can falling in love with a little twelve-year old girl keep affecting everything I do in life? "How can it be?" I guess I will never be able to understand or be able to explain how a simple suggestion from Polly could energize a chain reaction that would influence my thinking throughout life. For example, one day Polly suggested that I attend meetings of a group of Christian college young people, called the BSU. Of course a suggestion from Polly was just like an order to me. I did attend some of these meetings and later was elected president of the chapter. As president I was expected to attend the state convention of this organization. It was at this convention that I found myself walking the aisle to take the hand of the preacher. Many were dedicating their lives to be missionaries, preachers, and educational directors. All I could say was, "I want to dedicate my occupation, whatever it happens to be, to the Lord." A simple suggestion from Polly resulted in an action that later influenced most of the decisions of my life.

There were three letters from Polly in the two cigar boxes asserting that I must return to college after Uncle Sam no longer needed my services. Polly knew me too well. She seemed to know just exactly what to say in order to influence my actions. "Buddy, you must graduate from college. You have so much to offer the world." Now, I really did not know what I had to offer the world, but graduating from college became my number one goal in life.

One day I did earn a college diploma. I then became a life insurance salesman. I was an immediate success because I had been "selling" since I was eleven. However, there was a problem. After much prayer, the answer was clear that I was not to enjoy the prosperous life available at that time to college graduates. It seemed that God knew something about me that I did not know. Maybe He knew that if I did well financially, I would not be the servant He wanted me to be. It seemed I had the talent for making money, but every time I started to do well financially, God had another road for me to follow. The dedication of one's occupation to the Lord is dangerous business. This was the first of five career decisions in my life, and each resulted in a decrease in salary. All this happened because one day Polly made a suggestion to me.

I did not know exactly what God wanted me to do so I headed for graduate school at the University of Kentucky. At the end of the year I had completed all requirements for the master's degree. I had also used most of my savings and my G.I. bill benefits. I was really enjoying my graduate study, but it was time now for me to start earning money again. A large number of veterans were enrolling in college, and many small colleges were advertising for instructors. Because of the shortage of college teachers at this time, colleges were willing to employ teachers holding only the master's degree. I interviewed at two colleges and expected offers just as soon as they received references from my teachers. I began praying that God would help me select the right college for my first job. Well, God did help me, but not in the way I expected.

On Monday morning I had a note in my mail to report to the department head at the University of Kentucky as soon as possible. I did not know what I had done wrong, but I was in his office as soon as I could get an appointment. He looked over his horn-rimmed glasses, and stared at me for what seemed like a minute.

"Young man, some of your professors tell me you have applied for a job."

"Yes sir."

"Are you not challenged by graduate study?"

"Yes sir, I have enjoyed my graduate courses, but I have used all of my savings. I know you would give me an assistantship, but I cannot live on that amount of money."

"Well, three of your professors are on my back saying we cannot let you leave. They think you have the potential to earn the Ph.D. degree."

"Thank you, sir. I appreciate their confidence."

"If I could find a way to keep you in graduate school, would you be interested? Let me tell you up front that you would be working harder than you have ever worked in your life, probably harder than any person should work."

He then paused. I waited for him to explain, but he wanted my reaction. I finally said, "I think so."

"The dean has given me permission to employ three temporary instructors to handle the large number of returning

G.I.s this fall. I had assumed that we would steal three good teachers from local high schools. Instead, we have decided to employ two of our graduate students who have already completed several courses on their doctorates. Your professors are pushing me to offer this third position to you. You would teach a full load of five classes in addition to your graduate work. This is a terrible way to work on a doctorate, but your professors assure me that you can do it. Are you interested?"

"Yes sir!" I said calmly although I wanted to shout my reply. I remembered that Polly had assured me many times that I had something to offer the world in the way of service. In recent days it had seemed that this service was in the direction of college teaching. I also knew that colleges expected their teachers either to have doctorates or to be working on doctorates. In my prayer time that night I praised the Lord for providing an avenue to prepare for service in His kingdom. What was so amazing was that God had provided this when I was going in another direction.

Finally the ordeal was over. I had completed all work for the Ph.D. degree. Immediately, my thoughts were, "Polly should really be proud of me now. I am the first graduate of our small high school to earn this advanced degree." My professors at the University of Kentucky wanted their doctoral candidates to take jobs at prestigious universities in order to maintain their research programs. It was suggested that I interview at Florida State University and Virginia Polytechnic Institute. I was offered positions at both, and I chose Florida State.

I should have been happy at Florida State University, but something was wrong. I was well aware of the difficulty. I was not in God's will. It had been less than seven years since I had dedicated my occupation to the Lord, and somehow I had taken this job without His blessings. My pastor was certain

God was calling me to be a preacher. In fact, I think he made up excuses to be out of town so I would fill his pulpit while he was away. But God did not want me to be a preacher. He probably knew I would not be much of a preacher. What did God want from me? I prayed long and hard for direction. I was willing to go and do His will, but I had difficulty finding the answer.

Finally, it seemed that God was leading me to a small college in Birmingham, Alabama. I knew little about this college. Maybe it was better that way. Otherwise, I might not have been able to follow God's will. I did know it was a college that emphasized Christian values. God evidently wanted me to give my life to this type of institution.

I did not know that many of the buildings at this college were about to fall down, and that for many years the college had difficulty finding money to meet the payroll. The buildings were so dilapidated that occasionally a bit of plaster would fall from the ceiling onto either the floor or a student's head. Some faculty members joked that this was a new way of pounding knowledge into a student's head. At least it helped to keep students awake during boring lectures. Students joked that if the termites went to a convention, every building would collapse. Faculty salaries were exceedingly meager. A good portion of the college budget was being used to prepare for moving to a new campus. Faculty members complained that the new campus was being built with the salary increases they were not receiving.

All of the teachers in my department had desks in one large room of an old weather- boarded house with linoleum-covered floors. The house was named Oration Hall after the Speech Department located in one bedroom of the house. The prayer room for students was also in Oration Hall. The heat source was a gas space heater in each room, and the cooling system involved raising two windows and hoping for a breeze. In cold weather the first teacher to arrive in the office in the morning would light the space heater. The night watchman would light the gas grate in the Prayer Room very early in the morning. On real cold mornings, the first teacher to arrive usually had an urgent need for prayer.

My professors at the University of Kentucky wanted to know why anyone would leave an excellent position at Florida State University – a position involving upper division and graduate teaching, a position with unusual opportunities for advancement, a position with a good salary and an unbelievable increase promised for the next year – to teach at little known Howard College in Birmingham, Alabama. I knew the answer, and I smiled to myself because I was well aware that Polly had indirectly influenced this decision. I suspected she might still be directly influencing my life through her prayers. "Well Polly, this is the second time I have taken a salary decrease because of you."

Inwardly, at the end of the first year I was happy to be at Howard College. Outwardly, there were problems. Mainly, they were financial. By this time I was married to a wonderful person, and we were blessed with two small children. Both boys had health problems in our first years in Birmingham. Frequent doctor and hospital bills filled our mailbox. The medical program for Howard College faculty members at that time was basically nonexistent. For nine months teaching I received ten paychecks. Since summer school teaching was not available to new faculty members, we attempted to save one-fifth of each of the ten checks for July and August. We suddenly discovered that not only were we not saving for the two lean months, our bank account was decreasing a bit each month. This was not good.

We survived the first dreaded July and August because the Lord took care of our needs. I obtained a summer job at the Army Proving Grounds, Aberdeen, Maryland. For three months our family lived in an old dark apartment building in Aberdeen, but our pay each month was much larger than that I received from teaching. In spite of the fact that we traveled many weekends, we saved money each month at Aberdeen. Our bank balance was just about the same when we returned to Howard for the second year as it was at the beginning of the first year. An old country saying describes our situation, "We were holding our own."

I kept thinking, "What will we do next summer if I cannot find a summer job?" A true description of my thinking would have been, "Oh ye of little faith." I felt God should provide a "reasonable living" for a family trying to be in His will. My wonderful wife insisted we could live on less. I knew she was very economical, but I did not see how she could accomplish this miracle.

We prayed daily, "Lord, help us to turn our lives, our family, and our employment over completely to you. Then, Lord, help us to be satisfied and appreciative of what you arrange for our lives." I said the words without really meaning them. I wanted very much to be in God's will, but I did not want my family to suffer. In mid-fall, I finally was willing to accept whatever God had for me, however meager. Then God took over our finances.

A telephone call came to my office from a local aircraft corporation. The call began with a question, "Do you know anything about operations research?"

"Yes, I have some knowledge of this subject."

"Thank goodness! We have been unable to find anyone in Birmingham with knowledge of this subject. Could you use a little extra money by helping us a few hours each week?"

I wanted to shout, "Boy could I use it!" Instead I calmly said, "I think so, if I can be of help to you."

"When can you start, how many hours a week can you give us, and what rate of pay do you expect?"

"In all fairness to the college I should not work more than two afternoons a week, say Tuesdays and Thursdays. I have no idea of your pay scale."

"I'll meet you at the gate at 1:00 P.M. tomorrow (Thursday) with your temporary badge. We will pay you the highest engineering pay in our present contract with the Air Force. If you will start at this rate, we will insert your name as a consultant at a higher rate in the next Air Force contract."

I was estactic. Yes, we really needed the extra money for our family, but more than this we knew God was providing this opportunity because we were trying to be in His will. I said, "Wouldn't it be great if I could work full time with them next summer?" Not only did I work through the summer, the consulting work lasted for twelve years. Most of the time my assignments from NASA and the Air Force were way beyond my ability and training. Whenever it seemed that there was no way I could handle an assignment, I would remember what Polly had once said, "Buddy, you can do anything you want to do. Haven't you always accomplished the impossible?" (A copy is still in the old cigar box.) This encouraged me to work a little harder and pray a little longer. Always God seemed to help me find some solution.

The company was very good to me, increasing my consulting rate each year.When I was working full time in the summer, I was making good money. My only problem was they wanted me to work more than two afternoons a week. Finally they said, "Work at home at night as many hours as you wish and report your time once a week." I appreciated very much their faith in my honesty.

One day it dawned on my thick skull that my consultant pay was more than my salary for the work God wanted me to do. This was not right, but I was doing well financially. Working day and night, time passed so quickly. With its new campus Howard College grew very rapidly and became Samford University.

Many years ago, Polly wrote to me, "Buddy, we must keep growing both mentally and spiritually; otherwise we are dead." (Yes, a copy is in the old cigar box.) I knew immediately that I was guilty. I had been working so hard as a consultant, I was not growing academically.

Samford University had a sabbatical leave program. After six years of teaching, faculty members were eligible for a one-semester leave at full pay and a full year at half pay. On a sabbatical you could not do anything for which you received pay. That is, I had to make a choice between consulting work and a sabbatical. It seemed that by being very frugal, we could now live a normal life without the consulting pay so I applied for a sabbatical. The thought did run through my mind, "This is the third salary reduction I have taken on account of Polly."

What could I do that would catch the eye of the evaluating committee? I would have enjoyed some post-graduate work, but the boys were in critical years in school so we felt we could not leave the city. I had directed two National Science Foundation institutes for teachers and had a lot of notes, so I applied for a one-semester sabbatical to write a freshman mathematics textbook for liberal arts majors and teachers. The application was approved. I placed my typewriter on a card table in our unfinished basement and tried to write a book. I had no idea what I would do with the book, but I thought I might reproduce it and use it for one of my classes.

The more I wrote, the more I needed to write. Before I realized what was happening, the one semester book I had planned became a two-semester book. I worked so hard I began to dream that it might be published. With four copies of the manuscript in my suitcase, I headed for Miami, Florida, for the annual meeting of the Mathematical Association of America. I tried to remember all of my selling tricks that I had learned selling books and life insurance. I knew I needed these in order to persuade four editors to secure an evaluation of my manuscript. Most of the editors had not heard of Samford University. They were interested in authors from well-known schools.When I returned to Birmingham, I was minus four manuscripts. Four editors had agreed to submit my manuscript to reviewers. This was beyond my wildest dreams! Perhaps they were just trying to get rid of me.

As Polly once taught me, I did depend on the Lord as to whether this was the end of the trail for this manuscript. I was well aware that a very small percentage of manuscripts are accepted for print. At least I had had a sabbatical, and now I had good reference material for my classes.

To my surprise and joy, a reputable book company agreed to take the risk and publish the book. Enough copies were sold in two years for the book company to request that I rewrite the book for a second edition and have it ready for publication in two more years. The second edition sold more copies than any of its competitors, so there was to be a third edition. Sometime during the second edition there was a trip to California to receive a leather bound copy for the 100,000th book published. At the banquet, my editor, who later became president of the company, joked about the unknown author from an unknown college who talked him into looking at the manuscript. He felt that there was no way this manuscript would be published. (What he did not know was that the publication of this manuscript had been turned over to the Lord.) Every four years there was another edition: a third, a fourth, a fifth, and a sixth. The seventh and eighth editions were printed in two colors, leading to an award for the 400,000th book printed. The ninth edition was very expensive utilizing five colors. Then there was a tenth edition, and this year an eleventh edition. My wife said if she had known new editions would go on forever, she would have prayed that the first manuscript would not be published. Our son, Ed, shared the authorship with me on the last two editions. Working with him was an extra bonus. As I look back I realize this was God's way of blessing his servant who was trying to be in His will. The royalty payments made my total compensation at Samford competitive with the salaries at state universities.

As I return to my memories of Polly's influence on my life, I recall that many other things were missing at Howard College in 1953. After I had been on campus for a few weeks, I asked the department head about a typewriter, and the possibility of getting copies made of a test. What a shock! The department had no budget, no typewriter; you wrote your tests on a chalkboard with its many scratches and breaks. I must have been irritated because I gave a sharp answer, although I really liked my department head. "I prefer not to write my tests on a chalk board. My students expect me to put my test questions in a form where they can easily read them. I hope this shows my concern for my students."

"Well, if you insist on using something other than the chalk board, you will have to go see the Business Manager."

I had been on the job for only a few weeks and was irritated. This was not the time to go see the Business Manager. However, I was in his office, ready to insist on doing things right. This was my lucky day, which meant that God was taking care of my mistakes before I made them. The President had boasted a bit to his administrative staff about stealing a young professor from Florida State University, so the Business Manager wasn't about to upset this young professor during his first weeks on campus. He said the reason we did not have grading pencils, paper, a typewriter, reproduction equipment, a travel budget, and all those things usually associated with a department was that no one in the department had requested these things. Then he said, "Don't worry about it. Just go to the bookstore and purchase what you need and have the bill sent to my office. We have some old army-surplus typewriters, and I will have one delivered to your office. You are welcome to reproduce whatever you need in my office. Let me know what you need to spend on travel to a professional meeting, and I'll find some place to charge it."

When I would hear people criticize our Business Manager, I just could not understand. In my first encounter with him he seemed to care that I had concerns that needed attention. He continued to be a dear friend. With his meager resources, he always made an effort to meet my needs. I wonder what our relationship would have been if the Lord had not handled all the details in advance.

As I had dedicated my occupation to the Lord, it seemed that this included working with other members of the department to develop a strong mathematics program. During the first few years I was terribly disappointed because there seemed to be limited opportunities at Howard. However, little by little the Lord helped us to develop a strong mathematics faculty.

The Business Manager remembered his promise about travel to professional meetings. In the spring we had money for gasoline to attend the annual meeting of the Southeastern Section of the Mathematics Association of America. Two of us in the department attended this meeting, and we received money for one night in a motel. We had to buy our own meals, but that was satisfactory. Each year after this, at least one member of the faculty of the Mathematics Department attended this annual meeting. Evidently our method of advertising Samford was too slow, so the Lord took over. One day I was told that I had been selected to be Chairman of the Southeastern Section of the Mathematical Association of America. At this time most of the officers in this organization were from large universities. I had done nothing to deserve this honor, but I gladly accepted the responsibility as an avenue to advertise Samford University.

Another pressing need was to advertise the department to high schools. Many high school counselors, teachers, and students thought of Samford as a college for preachers. We had to let them know we had a strong program in mathematics. To advertise our program, we organized an "Invitational Mathematics Tournament for High School Students." The first year we invited teams from the high schools in close proximity to the college. The second year we invited all the high schools in Alabama, and the third year we included teams from surrounding states. A local insurance company was kind

218 / Polly's Influence On My Life

enough to donate money for prizes. High school students looked forward to the annual mathematics tournament. One part of the program involved "ciphering matches" with teammates encouraging participants. Students from all over the south became aware that Samford had an active mathematics program. It is possible that Samford (or Howard) had the first annual invitational mathematics tournament for high school students in the United States (at least the first with ciphering competition).

It was slow and difficult, but the Lord blessed our efforts to build a strong mathematics program. When the university decided to begin a graduate program, we were the first department to have a full class of graduate assistants. Recently the first graduating class with master's degrees in mathematics from Samford University had a reunion. It was great hearing of their success in life, and their service to the Lord.

Polly may have started it all, but I was truly happy in my work because I was serving students. I felt I was fulfilling God's will for my life. My pride and joy were my students. Through the years they continued to remember my love and concern for them as students, as well as my philosophy of life and my love for the Lord.

The Lord was always trying to find a place where I could serve Him best. As the years went by, I found myself serving as Head of the Mathematics Department, Chairman of the Division of Science and Mathematics, and then Dean of the Howard College of Arts and Sciences. In all of these positions I was able to continue my role as servant. This seemed to be what God, and also Polly, wanted for me.

Then God threw me a curve ball I had not expected. The university invited me to serve as Vice President for Academic Affairs. It was obvious to me that the university had an opportunity to become a truly outstanding institution with the right leadership. But God had called me to be a servant. Could one be a servant and at the same time a leader? I did not know the answer, so as Polly would have recommended, I placed everything in God's hands. My first reply was, "I do not want to leave teaching." I was told, "Don't worry. The average tenure in this academic office today across the United States is six years." I did not tell anyone, but I really did not want to lose the royalties on my five college textbooks that were now selling well, but God had other plans. I thought, "Here we go Polly, another salary decrease." I finally agreed to serve in this capacity, thinking that in about six years I would be back in the classroom. It was seventeen years before I returned to my first love, teaching college mathematics.

I really had given little thought about serving as head academic officer of a small university. I knew little about pharmacy, music, nursing, law, business, and education. When I met with the deans for the first time, I gave them my goals for the university. First, I expected each dean to provide dedicated leadership to improve the overall academic program of his/her school. I stated emphatically, "There's no place for second best in God's work." Then I requested that each dean spend a great deal of time finding ways to enhance Christian values in the academic programs of his/her school. I stated, "We are here to honor and glorify our Lord. Please remember this when you present to me a candidate for a teaching position in your school. If you will do these things, I will work hard for you, support you, and serve you to the best of my ability." Yes, I tried to provide leadership, but at the same time I knew I had been called by God to be a servant. I did not tell them that the only reason I considered serving as head academic officer was the opportunity to serve my Lord. I felt if they were observant they would see this immediately.

Because of my love for students, my appreciation for dedicated teachers, my loyalty to the university, and my desire that all work together cooperatively to honor the Lord by making Samford University into a great university, the Lord helped me to build a trust relationship with all components of the university. The deans cooperated, and it was great each year to see the university grow academically. At the same time it seemed that we were placing greater emphasis on Christian values.

The 1970s were difficult years for college administrators. I give God all the credit for protecting me. Somehow it became known at other universities of the state that Samford was not having the difficulties they were having. This led to an invitation to participate in a program of the Alabama section of the American Association of University Administrators. I wanted to say, "Depend on the Lord." But I knew that many would not understand. Instead I had to talk about what we were doing at Samford that might be different. Because of my love for students and my deep appreciation for dedicated faculty members, I did my best to keep open lines of communication. A weekly newsletter was sent to all faculty members from my office. All articles submitted were printed, even those critical of my office. The opportunity to express disagreements with the Vice President for Academic Affairs saved Samford from some disruptions that occurred at other universities.

Periodically I held "Coffee with the Veep" group meetings with faculty members on an informal basis, allowing them to ask any questions they had on their minds. If I did not know the answer, I promised to try to have an answer at the next "coffee."

My office was always open to students. I did my best to present their concerns to faculty committees. These actions, which did seem to be helpful during these difficult years, were not a result of my great administrative ability. They were a result of God's calling me to be a servant.

My participation on the program of the Alabama Chapter of University Administrators led to my being selected as president of this organization and later as the representative of private colleges on the Governor's Study Committee of the Alabama Commission on Higher Education. One thing led to another, and additional opportunities became available to advertise Samford University. There was no question that this small school was becoming a great university. There were two organizations of head academic officers associated with the Southern Association of Colleges: The Conference of Academic Deans of Southern States and The Southern Conference of Deans of Faculties and Academic Vice Presidents. The first organization was for small colleges and universities and the second for large universities. When I was asked to serve as President of the Conference of Academic Deans of Southern States, I thought it was a result of having many friends who were academic administrators in Alabama and many friends who were academic administrators at Baptist colleges. I must have been wrong. Three years later I was very surprised when I was asked to be President of the Southern Conference of

Deans of Faculties and Academic Vice-Presidents. Since no one had served previously as president of both organizations, I knew this had happened only because the Lord was providing a way for me to advertise Samford.

One day Polly wrote me:

> Buddy, the fact that you've had so many good things happen to you has not been due to luck, has it? Don't ever forget how good God has been to you. You have the talent and personality that can take you anywhere you want to go if you use it wisely and don't waste it. I'm looking forward to the time when you will be a worthwhile person in this world, and I have a feeling you won't disappoint me. Oh, no! I don't mean you will become famous. I mean you are going to make this world a better place to live.

You are right, Polly. God has been so good to me. It is amazing how God can mold one's life so it is useful to His kingdom if we are willing to follow His will for our lives. Forgive me, Lord, for being such a stubborn, cantankerous, self-centered, selfish country bumpkin. I'm sorry You had so much difficulty keeping me in Your will.

Thank you, Lord, for calling me to be a servant and for providing hundreds and hundreds of wonderful young people for me to serve. There is no question in my mind that many of them are today making this world a better place to live. Polly, you were some prophet many, many years ago.

Epilogue

To my dearest darling wife,

One day you said the reason you loved me was the many ways I had of surprising you. Well here is the biggest surprise of all. For our fifty-sixth wedding anniversary I have written a love story for you. As in any novel, all persons and names are fictional, with the exception of Polly and Buddy. These were the names we used when our love was growing so rapidly. We used these names as a reminder of when I first fell in love with you as a twelve-year-old freckle-faced girl.

Remember the day your mother found all that money in her Bible. She said it had to go, but I was stubborn and would not take the money. So we finally became engaged. Remember the beautiful wedding. Everything was decorated with magnolia blossoms.

God has been so good to us, giving us two sons: Ed, an outstanding college dean in Savannah, Georgia, and Paul, a prominent physician in Nashville, Tennessee. Our boys inherited my genes for selecting mates because now we have two wonderful daughters, Claire and Joy. Our five grandchildren, Aaron, Jodi, Brooke, Kate, and Mark, will really be surprised when they learn their grandpa has written a love story. They will probably say, "He should stick with mathematics books."

I love you,
Buddy Baskins